Alex's smile [barcode: P9-BIT-047] gaze piercing

"My name is Serina," she said, holding his eyes.

She wanted him to kiss the woman she was, not the public persona—serene princess, daughter of a long line of monarchs, scion of a defunct throne.

Tension sparked the silence between them, turning it heavy with desire.

"Do you know what you're asking for?" he said, a raw note altering the timbre of his voice and sending little shudders down her spine.

"Yes," she said. "Yes, I know. But what do *you* want?"

Something flickered in the burnished blue of his eyes and brought a half-mocking smile to that wicked mouth, with its narrow top lip buttressed by a sensuous lower one.

"A kiss," he said. "And I'm not asking, Serina— I'm taking what you've been silently promising me since we danced together at Gerd and Rosie's wedding."

He drew her toward him. She put a hand on his chest, looking up into an intense, chiseled face.

On a thrill that was half fear, half voluptuous anticipation, she thought he looked like a hunter….

ROBYN DONALD Greetings! I'm often asked what made me decide to be a writer of romances. Well, it wasn't so much a decision as an inevitable conclusion. Growing up in a family of readers helped; after anxious calls from neighbors driving down our dusty country road, my mother tried to persuade me to wait until I got home before I started reading the current library book, but the lure of those pages was always too strong.

Shortly after I started school, I began whispering stories in the dark to my two sisters. Although most of those tales bore a remarkable resemblance to whatever book I was immersed in, there were times when a new idea would pop into my brain—my first experience of the joy of creativity.

Growing up in New Zealand, in the subtropical north, gave me a taste for romantic landscapes and exotic gardens. But it wasn't until I was in my mid-twenties that I read a Harlequin® romance novel and realized that the country I love came alive when populated by strong, tough men and spirited women.

By then I was married and a working mother, but into my busy life I crammed hours of writing; my family has always been hugely supportive—even the various dogs who have slept on my feet and demanded that I take them for walks at inconvenient times. I learned my craft in those busy years, and when I finally plucked up enough courage to send off a manuscript, it was accepted. The only thing I can compare that excitement to is the delight of bearing a child.

Since then it's been a roller-coaster ride of fun, hard work and wonderful letters from fans. I see my readers as intelligent women who insist on accurate backgrounds along with an intriguing love story, so I spend time researching, as well as writing.

THE IMPOVERISHED PRINCESS

ROBYN DONALD

~ Rescued by the Rich Man ~

TORONTO NEW YORK LONDON
AMSTERDAM PARIS SYDNEY HAMBURG
STOCKHOLM ATHENS TOKYO MILAN MADRID
PRAGUE WARSAW BUDAPEST AUCKLAND

Recycling programs
for this product may
not exist in your area.

ISBN-13: 978-0-373-52826-4

THE IMPOVERISHED PRINCESS
Previously published in the U.K. as BROODING BILLIONAIRE,
IMPOVERISHED PRINCESS

First North American Publication 2011

Copyright © 2010 by Robyn Donald

This edition published by arrangement with Harlequin Books S.A.

For questions and comments about the quality of this book
please contact us at Customer_eCare@Harlequin.ca.

www.Harlequin.com

Printed in U.S.A.

THE IMPOVERISHED PRINCESS

CHAPTER ONE

NARROW-EYED, Alex Matthews surveyed the ballroom of the palace. The band had just played a few bars of the Carathian national folk song, a tune in waltz-time that was the signal for guests to take their partners for the first dance of the evening. The resultant rustle around the margins of the room flashed colour from the women's elaborate gowns and magnificent jewellery.

Alex's angular features softened a little when he saw the bride. His half-sister outshone any jewel, her blazing happiness making Alex feel uncomfortably like an intruder. Quite a few years younger, Rosie was the daughter of his father's second wife and, although they'd become friends over the past few years, he'd never had a close relationship with her.

Alex transferred his gaze to his brother-in-law of a few hours, the Grand Duke of Carathia. Gerd wasn't given to displays of overt emotion, but Alex blinked at the other man's unguarded expression when he looked down at the woman on his arm. It was as though there was no one in the room but the two of them.

It lasted scarcely a moment, just long enough for Alex to wonder at the subtle emotion that twisted inside him.

Envy? No.

Sex and affection he understood—respect and liking also—but love was foreign to him.

Probably always would be. The ability to feel such intense emotion didn't seem to be part of his character. And since breaking hearts wasn't something he enjoyed—a lesson he'd learned from a painful experience in his youth—he now chose lovers who could accept his essential aloofness.

However, although he couldn't imagine that sort of emotion in himself, he was glad his half-sister loved a man worthy of her, one who not only returned her ardour but valued her for it. Although he and Gerd were distant cousins, they had grown up more like brothers—and if anyone deserved Rosie's love, Gerd did.

Couples began to group around the royal pair, leaving them a space in the middle of the ballroom.

The man beside him said, 'Are you planning to sit this one out, Alex?'

'No, I'm pledged for it.' Alex's blue gaze moved to a woman standing alone at the side of the room.

Elegant and smoothly confident, Princess Serina's beautiful face revealed nothing beyond calm pleasure. Yet until Rosie and Gerd had announced their engagement, most of the rarefied circle of high society she moved in had assumed the Princess would be the next Grand Duchess of Carathia.

Regally inscrutable, if Serina of Montevel *was* secretly grieving she refused to give anyone the titillating satisfaction of seeing it. Alex admired her for that.

During the last few days he'd overheard several remarks from watchful wedding guests—a few compassionate but most from people looking for drama, the chance to see a cracked heart exposed.

Made obscurely angry by their snide spite, Alex mentally shrugged. The Princess didn't need his protection; her impervious armour of breeding and self-sufficiency deflected all snide comments, denied all attempts at sympathy.

He'd met her a year ago at Gerd's coronation ball, introduced by an elderly Spanish aristocrat who had formally reeled off her full complement of surnames. Surprised by a quick masculine desire, Alex had read amusement in the Princess's amazing, darkly violet eyes.

A little sardonically he'd commented on that roll call of blood and pride, power and position.

Her low amused chuckle had further fired his senses. 'If you had the same conventions in New Zealand you'd have a phalanx of names too,' she'd informed him with unruffled composure. 'They're nothing more than a kind of family tree.'

Possibly she'd meant it, but now, possessed of disturbing knowledge about her brother, Alex wasn't so sure. Doran of Montevel was only too aware that those names were embedded in European history. Did the Princess have any idea of what her younger brother had got himself mixed up with?

If she did she'd done nothing about it, so perhaps she also wanted to see herself back in Montevel, a true princess instead of the bearer of a defunct title inherited from her deposed grandfather.

And Alex needed to find out just what she did know. He set off towards her.

She saw him coming, of course, and immediately

produced an irritatingly gracious smile. The smoky violet of her gown echoed the colour of her eyes and hugged a narrow waist, displaying curves that unleashed something elemental and fierce inside Alex, an urge to discover what lay beneath that lovely façade, to challenge her on the most fundamental level—man to woman.

'Alex,' she said, the smile widening a fraction when he stopped in front of her. 'This is such a happy occasion for us all. I've never seen such a blissful bride, and Gerd looks—well, almost transfigured.'

A controlled man himself, Alex admired her skill in conveying that her heart wasn't broken. 'Indeed,' he responded. 'My dance, I believe.'

Still smiling, she laid a slender hand on his arm and together they walked into the waiting, chattering circle around Rosie and Gerd.

Alex glanced down, a phrase from childhood echoing in his head. *White as snow, red as blood, black as ebony.* Snow White, he remembered.

And Serina was an almost perfect snow princess.

Exquisite enough to star in a fairy tale, she radiated grace. Her black chignon set off her tiara and classical features perfectly, contrasting sensuously with the almost translucent pallor of her skin.

She'd passed on one part of the description, though; her lips were painted a restrained shade of dark, clear pink. A bold red would be too blatant, too provocative for this Princess.

But they were tempting lips…

A hunting instinct as old as time stirred into life deep within Alex. He'd wanted Serina Montevel ever since he'd first seen her, but because he too had wondered if she was wounded by dashed hopes he'd made no move to attract her attention. However, a year had passed—enough time to heal any damage to her heart.

He stopped with Serina on the edge of the crowd of dancers and sent a flinty territorial glance, sharp as a rapier, to a man a few paces away eyeing Serina with open appreciation. It gave him cold pleasure to watch the ogler hastily transfer his appreciative gaze elsewhere.

The band swung into the tune and the crowd fell silent as the newlyweds began waltzing. Softly the onlookers began to clap in time to the beat.

Serina glanced up, tensing when her eyes clashed with a sharp blue gaze. Her breath locked in her throat while she wrestled down an exhilarating excitement. Tall, dark and arrogantly handsome, Alex Matthews had a strangely weakening effect on her.

Warily, because the silence between them grew too heavy, almost significant, she broke into it with the first thing that came into her head. 'This is a very pretty tradition.'

'The Carathian wedding dance?'

'Yes.'

Neither Rosie nor Gerd smiled; eyes locked, it was as if they were alone together, absorbed, so intent on each other that Serina felt a sharp stab of—regret?

No, not quite. A kind of wistful envy.

Just over a year previously she'd decided to make it clear to Gerd—without being so crass as to say the words—that she wasn't on the market to become Grand Duchess of Carathia. Such a union would have solved a lot of her problems, and she admired Gerd very much, but she wanted more than a *convenient* marriage.

Just as well, because shortly afterwards Gerd had

taken one look at the Rosie he'd last seen as a child and lost his heart.

What would it be like to feel that herself? To be loved so ardently that even in public their emotions were barely containable?

Keeping her eyes on them, she said quietly, 'They fit, don't they.' It wasn't a question.

Alex's enigmatic glance, as polished as the steel-sheen on a sword blade, brought heat to her skin. What a foolish thing to say about a couple who'd just made their wedding vows!

Of course they fitted. For now, anyway, she thought cynically. Somewhere she'd read that the first flush of love and passion lasted two years, so Gerd and Rosie would enjoy perhaps another year of this incandescent delight in each other before it began to fade.

'Perceptive of you,' Alex commented in a level voice. 'Yes, they fit.'

The music swelled, accompanied by a whirl of colour and movement as everyone joined in the dance, swirling around the absorbed couple.

Serina braced herself. Nerves taut, she rested one hand on Alex's shoulder and felt his fingers close around the other as he swung her into the waltz. Anticipation sizzled through her—heady, compelling, so unnerving that after a few steps she stumbled.

Alex's arm clamped her against his lean, athletic body for breathless seconds before he drawled, 'Relax, Princess.'

His warm breath on her skin sent tiny, delicious shudders through her, a gentler counterpoint to the sultry heat that burgeoned deeply within her at the intimate flexing of his thigh muscles. Shocked by the immediacy of her response, Serina pulled herself a safe distance away and forced herself to ignore the sensual tug until her natural sense of rhythm settled her steps.

This acute physical response—jungle drums of sensation pounding through her—had sprung into action the first time she'd met Alex. Gritting her teeth, she resisted the tantalising thrill, sharp and adrenalin-charged as though she faced a sudden danger.

Did he feel the same?

She risked an upward glance, heart racing into overdrive when she met searing, disturbingly intent eyes. His grip didn't tighten, but she sensed a quickening in him that he couldn't control.

Yes, she thought triumphantly, before a flurry of panic squelched that intoxicating emotion.

Swallowing, she said in her most remote tone, 'Sorry. I wasn't concentrating.'

Then wondered uneasily if the admission had hinted at her body's wilful blooming.

Rapidly she added brightly, 'This has been one of the most charming weddings I've ever attended. Rosie is so happy, and it's lovely to see Gerd utterly smitten.'

'Yet you seem a little distracted. Is something worrying you?' Alex enquired smoothly.

Well, yes—several things, in fact, with one in particular nagging at her mind.

But Alex wasn't referring to her brother. He'd have noticed that plenty of eyes around the ballroom were fixed on her, some pitying, others malicious. Of the two she preferred the spite, although a hissed aside that had been pitched carefully to reach her ears still stung.

'It must be like eating bitter aloes for her,' a French duchess had said.

Her blonde companion had returned on a laugh, 'I'll bet the brother's furious—once she failed to land Prince Gerd they lost their best chance of clawing their way out of poverty. And losing out to a nobody must be bitter indeed.'

Not everyone was as catty, but she'd noticed enough abruptly terminated conversations and parried enough speculative glances to know what many of the guests were thinking.

Let them think what they liked! Pride stiffening her spine, she smiled up at Alex. Oh, not too widely, in case those watchers suspected her of acting—but with a slow, amused glimmer that should give some of the eager gossipers a few seconds of thought.

'I'm not distracted, and nothing's wrong,' she told him, her tone level and deliberate.

His black brows climbed for a second. 'As you've probably noticed, quite a few people here are wondering whether you're regretting a missed opportunity.'

At least he'd come out and said it. She tilted her head and met his calculating scrutiny with unwavering steadiness, praying he couldn't see how brittle she was beneath the surface self-possession.

'About as much as Gerd is,' she returned coolly, hoping she'd banished every trace of defiance from her voice.

Alex's mouth—unsoftened by its compelling hint of sensuality—relaxed into a smile that was more challenge than amusement. 'Indeed?'

'Indeed,' she returned, infusing the word with complete assurance.

'Good.'

She shot him a questioning glance, parrying a look

that sent a quiver the full length of her spine. He let his gaze wander across her face, finally settling it on her lips. A voluptuous excitement smouldered through her.

Surely—yes, she thought with a triumph so complete she could feel it radiating through her—he was *flirting* with her. And she was going to respond.

But first she had to know something. That suspect recklessness gave her the courage to say, 'I'm surprised you're alone this week.'

His latest reputed lover was a gloriously beautiful Greek heiress, quite recently divorced. Rumour had it that Alex had been the reason for the marriage breakup but Serina found that difficult to believe. He was noted for an iron-bound sense of integrity, and it seemed unlikely he'd let a passing fancy for a beautiful woman compromise that.

However, she thought with another spurt of cynicism, what did she really know about him? Nothing, except that he'd used his formidable intelligence, ruthless drive and an uncompromising authority to build a worldwide business empire.

Besides, his fancy for his Greek lover might not be passing.

Alex's tone was matter-of-fact. 'Why? I have no partner or significant other.'

So that was that. *Neither have I* seemed far too much like a bald, much too obvious invitation.

Serina contented herself with a short nod, and kept her eyes fixed on the throng whirling behind him. He was an excellent dancer, moving with the lithe, muscular grace of an athlete, and wearing his formal clothes with a kind of lethal elegance that proclaimed the powerful body beneath.

'So what's ahead for you?' Alex asked coolly. 'More of the same?'

'More weddings? No one else I know is getting married in the immediate future,' she returned, deflecting the query.

He met her glance with a glinting one of his own. 'You're happy just doing the social round?'

A little shortly, Serina replied, 'Actually, I'm planning to go back to school.'

Alex's gaze sharpened. 'You surprise me. I thought you'd settled into being Rassel's muse.'

'We decided he needed a new one,' she told him without rancour.

Her time with the up-and-coming Parisian fashion designer had been stimulating but, although losing the very generous salary was a blow, she'd been relieved when he'd decided he needed someone more edgy, more in tune with his new direction.

She had no illusions. Rassel had originally chosen her because she had the entrée to the circles he aspired to. The fact that she both photographed well and possessed the body to display his clothes superbly had helped him make the decision. It had always been a problematic relationship; although Rassel referred to her as his muse he'd expected her to behave like a model, and had only reluctantly accepted any input from her. Now that he'd made his reputation he didn't need her any more.

And she didn't miss his monstrous ego or his insecurity.

Alex asked, 'So what are you going to study? Horticulture?'

Did he know she wrote a column on gardens?

'Landscape architecture.'

She was so looking forward to it. She'd just come into a small inheritance from her grandfather, the last King of Montevel. Added to the money she earned for the column, the bequest would provide enough money for Doran to finish university as well as pay her tuition fees and living expenses.

It would mean an even more rigorous routine of scrimping, but she was accustomed to that.

'I suppose that figures. Will you continue writing your garden column for that celebrity magazine?' Alex's dismissive tone made it quite clear what he thought of the publication.

'Of course.' Loyalty to the editor made her enlarge on her first stiff response. 'They took a chance on me and I've always done my best to live up to their expectations.'

Why on earth was she justifying herself to this man? She tried to ignore a turbulent flutter beneath her ribs when she parried his enigmatic gaze.

'Why landscape architecture? It's a far cry from writing about pretty flowers and people who never get their hands dirty.'

Allowing a hint of frost to chill her words, she said, 'Apart from admiring the beauty of what they achieve, I respect the hopeless, impossible ambition of gardeners, their desire to create a perfect, idealised landscape—to return to Eden.' Crisply she finished, 'And I'll be good at it.'

'Your title and social cachet will see that you succeed.'

The comment, delivered in a negligent voice, hurt her. Especially since she knew there was an element of truth to it.

Serina hid her stormy gaze with long lashes. 'It will help. But to succeed I'll need more than that.'

'And you think you have whatever it takes?'

'I know I have,' she said calmly.

For answer he pulled her hand into a suitable position for inspection. 'Perfect skin,' he murmured on a sardonic note. 'Not a scratch or stain anywhere. Immaculately manicured nails. I'll bet you've never got your hands dirty.'

The corners of her mouth curved upwards and her eyes glittered. 'How much will you wager?'

Alex's laugh smashed through defences already weakened by the feel of his arms around her and the subtle connection with his body, the brush of his thighs against her, the barely discernible scent that seemed to be a mixture of soap and his own inherent male essence.

'Nothing,' he said promptly, returning her hand to its normal position. 'If you want to gamble you shouldn't show your hand so obviously. Did you have a flower garden as a child?'

'I did, and a very productive vegetable plot. My mother believed gardening was good for children.'

His expression gave nothing away. Hard-featured, magnetic, he was far too handsome—and Serina was far too aware of his dangerous charisma.

He said, 'Of course, I should have remembered that your parents' garden on the Riviera was famous for its beauty.'

'Yes.' Her mother had been the guiding light behind that. Working in her garden had helped soothe her heart whenever her husband's affairs figured in the gossip columns.

The property had been sold after her parents' deaths,

gone like everything else to pay the debts they'd left behind.

The music drew to an end, and Alex loosened his strong arm about her, looking down with a smile that was pure male challenge. 'You should come to New Zealand. It has fascinating plants, superb scenery and some of the best gardens in the world.'

'So I believe. Perhaps one of these days I'll get there.'

'I'm going back tomorrow. Why not come with me?'

Startled, she flashed him a glance, wondering at his unexpectedly keen scrutiny. Why on earth had he suggested such a crazy thing? Yet she had to resist a fierce desire to take him up on his offer—and on whatever else he was offering.

Just pack a small bag and go...

But of course she couldn't. Reluctantly she said, 'Thank you very much but no, I can't just head off like that, however much I might want to.'

'Is there anything keeping you on this side of the world? An occasion you don't dare miss?' He paused before drawling, 'A lover?'

Colour flared briefly in her cheeks. A lover? No such thing in her life—ever.

'No,' she admitted reluctantly. 'But I can't just disappear.'

'Why not? Haruru—the place I own in Northland—is on the coast, and if you're interested in flora there's a lot of bush on it.' When she looked at him enquiringly he expanded, 'In New Zealand all forest is called bush. And in Northland, my home, botanists are still discovering new species of plants.'

He smiled down at her with such charm that for a

charged moment she forgot everything but a highly suspicious desire to go with him.

It was high summer, and the small, cheap apartment in the back street of Nice was stuffy and hot, the streets crowded with tourists... Photographs she'd seen of New Zealand had shown a green country, lush and cool and mysterious.

But it was impossible. 'It sounds wonderful, but I don't do impulse,' she returned lightly.

'Then perhaps it's time you did. Bring your brother, if you want to.'

If only! Temptation wooed her, fogging her brain and reducing her willpower to a pale imitation of its normal robust self.

A trip to New Zealand might divert Doran from his increasingly worrying preoccupation with that wretched video game he and his friends were concocting. Prone to violent enthusiasms, he usually lost interest as quickly as he'd found it, but his fascination with this latest pursuit seemed to be coming worryingly close to an addiction. Serina had barely seen him during the past few months.

A holiday could wean him away from it.

It suggested a way for her to avoid the frustration of these past months, too. The sly innuendoes and unspoken sympathy, the rudeness of media people demanding to know how she felt now that her heart was supposedly shattered, the downright lies written about her in the tabloids—it had all been getting to her, she admitted bleakly.

If she went to New Zealand with Alex Matthews her world would assume they were lovers. How she'd enjoy hurling a supposed affair in every smug, avid face! A sharp, clamouring excitement almost persuaded her to agree.

For a moment she wavered, only to rally at the return of common sense. Just how would that prove she wasn't hiding a broken heart or shattered hopes?

It wouldn't. The gossips would accurately peg it as bravado, and therefore further confirmation of their suspicions.

'That's very kind of you,' she said carefully, 'and I'm sure Doran would love to visit New Zealand.'

'But?' Alex said ironically.

'We can't afford a holiday right now.'

Broad shoulders lifted in a slight shrug, but his gaze didn't waver. 'I share a jet with Kelt and Gerd, so transport won't be a problem. And I have an appointment in Madrid in a month's time, so I could drop you both off at Nice on the way there.' He looked down, eyes glinting, and challenged softly, 'Scared, Princess?'

'My name is Serina,' she stated, tipped off balance by the cynical note in his voice. 'What reason do I have to be afraid?'

Apprehensive, yes. Her stomach felt as though she were standing on the edge of a high cliff. Alex Matthews was way out of her league. Yet Doran...

She looked across the ballroom to her brother, laughing with a group of young men, one of whom was his greatest friend, the son of an old associate of her father's, another exile from Montevel. It was young Janke who'd introduced Doran to the excitement of computer gaming. Together they'd come up with the idea of creating their own game and making a fortune by selling the rights.

It would be a huge success, Doran had told her enthusiastically, and sworn her to secrecy in case any other video game creator got wind of their idea and stole it.

At first she'd dismissed it as an amusing fantasy on their part—until the project had taken over Doran's life.

A month on the other side of the world might just break the spell.

Alex said bluntly, 'You have nothing to fear from me.'

Colour heated her skin. 'I know that,' she said on a note that probably sounded a bit equivocal.

As though she hadn't spoken, he went on, 'And accommodation won't be a problem—I live in a huge old Victorian house with enough bedrooms for a huge Victorian family. As well as being beautiful, Northland is interesting in itself—the first place where Maori and Europeans met and mingled and clashed.'

The hairs on the back of her neck lifted in a primitive reaction to...what?

Nothing, she told herself curtly. Although Alex's tone was pleasant, it was also impersonal, and his offer to host Doran as well meant he didn't expect her to fall into his bed.

Well, not right away...

Nerves zinging, she said, 'It's just not possible,' and dismissed the subversive thought that a month in New Zealand would provide her with photographs and information for quite a few columns.

But Alex must have noticed that moment of weakness because he said, 'Why not?' And when she hesitated he went on, 'Why don't you ask your brother how he feels?'

He'd refuse, she was sure. 'OK, I'll do that.'

She sent another look across the room, intercepted by her brother, who strode across to them, lean and athletic-looking for someone who'd spent most of the past six months in front of a computer.

When Alex casually mentioned his suggestion Doran responded with his usual enthusiasm. 'Of course you must go, Serina!'

'The invitation is for you too,' Alex said pleasantly.

Excitement lit up Doran's mobile face, then faded. He glanced at Serina before saying, 'I wish I could, but... you know how it is.' He spread his hands and finished vaguely, 'Appointments, you see.'

Alex said, 'I believe you're interested in diving.'

'Well, yes.' Doran's eager response was a sharp contrast to his previous tone.

'New Zealand has some fantastic sites—in fact, there are two magnificent wrecks not far from Haruru, but friends of mine are going up to Vanuatu in the Pacific to dive the reefs. If you're interested I'm sure I could get you a berth.'

Doran's look of extreme longing increased almost comically when Alex added, 'They're talking about diving the Second World War wrecks there, as well.'

Serina said quickly, 'Wouldn't you have to be an experienced diver to deal with those?'

'Serina—'

Doran's protest was overridden by Alex's voice. 'So what are your qualifications, Doran, and where have you dived?'

Doran launched into his CV and, when he'd run down, Alex said, 'That sounds good enough.' He looked at Serina and added with a smile that held more than a tinge of irony, 'And, just to reassure your anxious sister, my friends are responsible and expert divers and I'm sure you're sensible.' He mentioned the name of a family famed for their exploration of the seas and the subsequent prize-winning television programmes.

'Wow! And I'm a very cautious diver!' Doran said, clearly forgetting that he'd refused the trip. He flashed an indignant glance at his sister. 'You know that, Serina.'

She blinked. She'd had to learn thrift since her parents' death, so that now the easy way the very rich moved around the world startled her, and the smoothly masterful way Alex had taken control of the situation made her feel the ground had been cut from under her feet.

'Of course you are,' she said, 'but you'd have to get to Vanuatu, and we can't possibly impose—'

Alex cut her short. 'Doran won't be imposing. My friends are taking up a yacht.' He glanced at the man beside him. 'You'll probably have to work your passage.'

Cheerfully, Doran said, 'That's no problem.'

Without looking at Serina, Alex said casually, 'I'll be leaving tomorrow morning. Let me know when you've made up your mind. And now, if you'll excuse me, I'd better go and see whether Gerd needs me for anything.'

CHAPTER TWO

BARELY waiting long enough for Alex to walk out of hearing, Doran said defiantly, 'Serina, don't be so damned *responsible*. I'm an adult, you know, legally and in every other way. The diving in Vanuatu is absolutely fantastic, and since you let Gerd slip through your fingers this will probably be the only chance I'm ever likely to get to see it.'

Serina returned acidly, 'I thought you were going to make your fortune with your wretched game!'

And could have kicked herself for letting his angry response get to her. Her brother loved her, but he needed a more mature figure in his life, someone he would respect and listen to.

Shamefaced, he admitted, 'OK, I was completely out of order and unfair. I'm sorry. But...' The words trailed away.

'Anyway, you told Alex you couldn't go,' she reminded him.

He sent her a look of mingled exasperation and embarrassment. 'It's too good a chance to miss. I can organise it.'

Relieved, she retorted, 'In that case, you'd be mad not to take Alex up on his offer.'

'So would you,' he said.

They measured glances. It looked as though he'd refuse if she did.

Surrendering, Serina shrugged and said lightly, 'Fair enough. I've always wanted to see New Zealand, and it would be a fantastic opportunity to find material for the column.'

'Oh, for heaven's sake, Serina, loosen up a bit! Forget the column and being a big sister—just have a proper holiday. Give Alex Matthews a chance to show you how much easier life can be when you're not trying so hard to be a role model.'

That hurt, but she smiled and said coolly, 'Perhaps I might.'

Watching him stride away, she asked herself why she wasn't exulting that—thanks to Alex's unexpected offer—things had fallen into place so easily.

Instead, she found Doran's final comment running around in her mind.

Fun? With Alex Matthews? She looked across to where he stood talking to the royal couple. Her gaze roved his face, unconsciously noting the strong framework, the lean body in superbly tailored evening clothes, the formidable, arrogantly effortless impact of his presence.

Tingles of sensation shortened her breath and hastened her pulse. He impressed her altogether too much, and that could be dangerous.

Of course, on closer acquaintance they might decide they didn't like each other...

Serina dragged in an unsteady breath, feeling as though she'd been caught up in a storm, tossed and tumbled by strong winds until she didn't know where she was going. *Liking* had nothing to do with the stark fact that whenever she saw Alex Matthews—or even thought of him—something shifted in the pit of her stomach and she felt a strange mixture of wariness and elation as her hormones raged out of control.

If she went to New Zealand she suspected she'd be even more vulnerable. Could she subdue this elemental response, leash it so she'd return unscathed after a month of close contact?

Put like that, it sounded idiotically Victorian—just like the mansion Alex lived in.

She didn't have to go. Doran had clearly decided to take up his offer. She could turn his invitation down, retreat to normality...

And spend the rest of her life wondering if she'd been a complete coward.

Controlling an urge to gnaw her lip indecisively, she greeted an approaching couple with relief. But later in the evening she found herself face to face with someone she'd successfully avoided until then. Superbly dressed, the older woman was still beautiful enough to dazzle.

As she had dazzled Serina's father.

Her mother's anguish only too vividly remembered, Serina masked her dislike and contempt with a calm smile as the woman cooed, 'My dear girl, this must be *such* a difficult time for you.' Her words oozing an odious sympathy that clashed with her avid scrutiny, she went on, 'I do so admire your courage in coming here.'

Serina held onto her temper with a stoic determination she hoped didn't show in her face. 'You are too complimentary—I can assure you it took no courage.'

The older woman sighed. 'Such noble defiance,' she

said patronisingly. 'So like your dear father—he clung to that magnificent aristocratic pride even when he'd lost everything. One could only admire his spirit in the face of such tragedy, and wish that he had been rewarded for it.'

Furious at the mention of her father, Serina couldn't trust herself to speak, so raised her brows instead.

The older woman went on, 'And for you, I hope that soon the pangs of being rejected will ease. A broken heart is—' She broke off abruptly, her gaze darting behind and above Serina.

The back of Serina's neck prickled and she had to stop herself from twisting around. She knew who'd come up behind her.

A warm smile pulled up the corners of the older woman's impossibly lush mouth. 'Mr Matthews,' she purred, 'how lovely to see you.' Her tone was deep, slightly husky, and somehow she imbued the meaningless words with an undercurrent of sexuality.

A sizzle of emotion tightened Serina's face, caused by something that came humiliatingly close to jealousy. She half-turned and met Alex's hard blue gaze. After a second he looked away and greeted the older woman with aloof courtesy.

Her father's mistress cooed, 'As I was about to tell the Princess, repining is such a waste of time, but I see I have no need to bore her with lessons learnt over a lifetime. Clearly she has already packed away the past and is looking to the future.'

Serina met her smug smile with a stiff movement of her head. 'So kind of you to take an interest in my life,' she said, disgust and anger edging her words. How dared the woman insinuate that she was chasing Alex?

Smoothly, Alex said, 'I'm sure you'll excuse us, madam. The Grand Duke and Duchess wish to speak to the Princess before they leave.'

As they walked away Serina said stiffly, 'You didn't need to rescue me; I can cope.'

'I'm sure you can,' he said, a sardonic smile tilting his hard, beautiful mouth, 'but I dislike vultures on principle. They foul the atmosphere.'

Serina gave a shocked gasp, followed by a choke of laughter. 'She's a horrid woman, but that's really too harsh.'

'It's not. You are far too polite.'

A raw note in the words made her look up sharply. After the slightest of pauses he went on, 'I like that little gurgle of laughter. I don't think I've heard it before.'

'I don't do it to order,' she retorted, furious because she was flushing. What was it about this man that turned her into some witless idiot?

'Careful,' Alex warned, his voice amused. 'The mask is slipping.'

Serina faltered. The hand beneath her elbow gripped hard enough to keep her upright, and for a second she wondered if she'd have bruises there tomorrow.

'The mask?' she enquired stiffly.

'The one you wear all the time—the perfect-princess mask that hides the puppet behind,' he returned with cool insolence, relaxing his grip.

Was that how he saw her—a lifeless *thing* hiding behind a disguise?

Squelching a foolish stab of pain, she stated, 'I'm not really a princess—Montevel is now a republic so it's just another empty title. And surely you must know that nobody is perfect.'

'So what's behind that utterly poised, totally collected, exceedingly beautiful face?'

Her startled glance clashed with an assessing scrutiny that sent a shiver scudding down her spine. 'A very ordinary person,' she countered, hoping she sounded more composed than she felt.

A very ordinary person still fuming over the exchange with her father's mistress—and secretly thrilled by Alex's cool summary of her attributes.

Thankfully they'd reached the royal couple, and Alex drawled, 'Rosie, Gerd, tell Serina she'll love New Zealand. I don't think I've entirely convinced her that it's worth crossing half the world to see.'

The brand-new Grand Duchess smiled up at Serina, her vivid face alight. 'Of *course* you'll love it,' she said, her pride in her country obvious. 'It's the most beautiful country in the world—apart from Carathia. And as a Northlander born and bred, I'm convinced that Northland is the best part of it.'

'Everyone says it's glorious,' Serina said, very aware of Gerd's speculative glance.

Enthusiastically, Rosie continued, 'And Haruru is just—magical. Huge and green and with beaches that match anything the Mediterranean offers.' She and her new husband exchanged an intimate smile that indicated a shared experience.

Serina stifled another pang of envy.

Blandly, Alex said, 'Gerd, perhaps you can reassure the Princess that she'll be perfectly safe staying with me.'

Embarrassed by his bluntness, Serina sent him a furious glance and blurted, 'I didn't think—' She caught herself and finished more sedately, 'Of course I know that!'

Gerd's brows lifted and the two men exchanged a look, a masculine thrust and parry that made Serina wonder. Although Alex and the Grand Duke didn't look alike, for a second the resemblance between them outweighed the differences.

Then Gerd said levelly, 'You can trust Alex.'

'I'll second that,' Rosie said with conviction, adding with a wry laugh, 'Even when he's being a pain in the neck—actually, *especially* when he's being a pain in the neck—he's utterly staunch.'

Grabbing at her composure, Serina said, 'I'm quite sure he is.' She took in a swift breath and managed to smile. 'I'm just not accustomed to making such quick decisions.'

They spoke for a few more minutes, then she wished them all happiness, and Alex escorted her back. Halfway across the expanse of floor, he said, 'So are you coming to New Zealand or not?'

'Yes,' she snapped, making up her mind with jarring suddenness.

Lapis lazuli eyes held hers for a tense moment before Alex nodded. 'You'll enjoy it—and think of the columns you'll be able to source. I'm leaving at ten tomorrow morning, so I'll see you get a wake-up call in time.'

Serina's fingers trembled as she fastened her seat belt. She'd used cosmetics to hide the toll a sleepless night had taken on her face, but nothing could smooth away the turmoil of thoughts and emotions knotting her stomach.

The previous night, raw from her encounter with her

father's mistress and Doran's words, it had been easy to be defiant, but once the ball was over and Rosie and Gerd had been farewelled in showers of rose petals, she'd gone to her room wondering why on earth she'd let her dislike of the woman manoeuvre her into a decision she might come to regret.

And there had been a couple of shocks since then, the first when Alex had told her that Doran had left for Vanuatu halfway through the night.

'Why?' she demanded in the car that was taking her and Alex to the airport.

'When I contacted my friends last night they told me they were already there, and almost ready to leave for the diving sites, so I got Doran to organise his own journey. He managed to talk himself onto several flights that will get him there within their deadline.'

She gave him a look of astonishment mingled with indignation. Doran had always relied on her to organise any travel arrangements. And who was paying his fare? A sick apprehension clutched at her.

As though he could read her mind, Alex said blandly, 'Don't worry about finances. Doran and I worked it out between us.'

'How?' she demanded.

'He's going to spend his holidays for the next year working for me,' Alex told her calmly.

'Working for you?' This time she felt a mixture of bewilderment and relief. If Doran was working for Alex he wouldn't have time to sit in front of a computer dreaming up fairy-tale fantasies of derring-do that might—but probably wouldn't—earn him a fortune.

'There's always something to be done in an organisation like mine,' Alex told her.

She eyed him sharply. 'Why are you doing this for him?'

'He was desperate to get to Vanuatu, and this seemed the best way to achieve that.'

'It's very kind of you,' she said with reserve.

'I'm not particularly kind,' he corrected her, 'but I don't like to make an offer and then have to retract it. This way he'll get the holiday he wants, and he'll also see a bit of the world. As for working for me—I assume he's going to have to earn his living?'

'Of course.'

'Then the experience will give him an idea of how the corporate and business worlds are organised.'

Serina had barely digested this when she discovered that Gerd's brother Kelt and his family weren't travelling with them.

Surprised anew, she said, 'I thought—somehow I assumed they were going home with us—with you.'

He shook his head. 'They're flying to Moraze to spend some time with his in-laws.'

She'd watched Alex with his cousin's small children, surprised and rather touched by their patent pleasure in his company. And his obvious affection for them hinted at a softer side to the man.

She'd looked forward to seeing more of them. But she and Alex would be alone—or as alone as anyone could be on a plane that boasted more flight crew than passengers.

A rebellious excitement welled up, so keen she could feel it thrilling through every cell. She, Serina Montevel, who'd never done a reckless thing in her life, was heading for a holiday on the other side of the world with a man she found wildly attractive.

Although *attractive* was far too pallid and emotionless a word. A sensible woman would have refused his invitation—would have kept on saying no until Alex decided she was more bother than she was worth...

Serina realised she was exceedingly glad that she wasn't that sensible woman.

Alex broke into her scattered thoughts with a question. 'Are you a nervous flier?'

'No,' she told him decisively, adding, 'This is all new to me. I've never been in a private jet before.'

A black brow climbed. 'You surprise me.'

'Why?'

He leaned back and regarded her with enigmatic eyes. 'I had the impression you spent a lot of time jetting around the royal circuit.'

'Usually I drive,' she told him evenly. Sometimes she used trains. It irritated her—no, it *hurt*—that he should despise her without bothering to take the trouble of finding out anything about her.

She went on, 'And I've never crossed the world before. Is jet lag as bad as they say?'

'Some people find it very difficult to deal with. I don't.'

'Ah, an iron man,' she said sweetly.

His smile was swift and unexpected, sending a reckless shiver of pleasure through Serina.

'Did I sound smug?' he asked. 'I'm fortunate, but I do take precautions.'

'Such as?'

'I always change my watch to the time of my destination.' He extended an arm to show her.

Automatically, Serina noted the watch—a superb brand, classic and without ostentation. She dragged her gaze from that sinewy wrist, rejecting the memory of how strong it was. When she'd faltered he'd held her upright without any visible effort. And yes, he'd marked her. The bruises were faint and would soon fade, but she felt oddly as though she'd been branded.

'New Zealand is nine hours ahead of us, and from now on we'll be eating at that time,' Alex told her. 'If you can relax enough to sleep later, you'll have adjusted to the local time when we arrive in Auckland.'

Sleeping wouldn't be difficult. She'd spent a lot of last night staring into the darkness and wondering what on earth she'd agreed to.

Nothing, she told herself again. After all, Alex's attitude, as well as his remark to Gerd and Rosie the previous night, had made it obvious that he was fully in control of his physical urges. Which had to be a good thing…

It was a pity she couldn't quite feel any gratitude for his unspoken promise of restraint.

She bent her head and altered her watch to match his, saying, 'Rosie says she drinks gallons of water and tries to spend at least ten minutes every hour walking or doing exercises.'

She'd been grateful for that information; at least striding around the cabin would give her something to do, something to concentrate on.

Not that drinking a lake of water or walking the whole way to New Zealand would slow the pace of her heart, or stop her from being so acutely, intensely aware of

Alex she felt as though she was inhaling his essence with every breath she took.

'Keeping away from alcohol and caffeine seems to help too,' Alex told her laconically.

'That won't be a problem.'

However, when the engines changed note and they began to pick up speed down the runway, Serina decided she could use something strong and sustaining. Dry-mouthed, she peered out at the mountains of Carathia rapidly speeding past as the jet broke free of the earth and started to climb.

A weird, baseless panic clenched her stomach muscles. Deliberately, carefully, she relaxed them and kept her eyes fixed on the view outside.

Never in all her life had she behaved so impetuously. *Never*. Thinking back, she couldn't remember when she'd decided that the best way to meet life was with restraint and cool composure. Possibly she'd just been born sensible and prosaic.

Whatever the cause, having been her mother's confidante in the continuing saga of unfaithfulness and despair that had been her parents' marriage, she'd vowed that she wasn't going to endure pain like that. So far, no man had ever been able to test that decision.

Yet Alex's caustic comparison of her to a puppet had been the final impetus that stung her into jettisoning caution and common sense to take this wild step into the unknown.

Alex leaned back in his seat and smiled at her. Her heart jumped and she relished an intoxicating sense of freedom. Half scared, half excited, she admitted that Doran had been right.

Unless she wanted to wear the princess mask for the

rest of her life, she needed to break out and find out who the real Serina was. Restraint and reserve could go hang. While she was in New Zealand she'd be the perfectly ordinary woman she'd told Alex she was.

A sudden lightness, almost a feeling of relief, sent her spirits soaring. All her life she'd been an appendage to something or someone else—the daughter of her parents, Doran's sister, the last Princess of Montevel, cousin to every royal family in Europe.

Even her career… Although she'd proved she was a good writer with a gift for painting the essence of a landscape in words, it had been her title—and the entrée it gave her—that got her the chance to write her first column.

Keeping her eyes fixed on the view through the window, she watched as, still climbing steeply, the plane wheeled and turned away from the Europe she knew so well, heading towards unknown, more primal shores on the other side of the world.

When the seat belt light flicked off Alex touched her arm—the lightest of touches, yet it ran like wildfire through her.

He said, 'I have work to do. If you need anything, ring for the steward.'

She nodded, watching him surreptitiously as he moved across to a desk that had clearly been set up for business. Tall and rangy, the chiselled planes and angles of his face strong and disturbingly sensual, he dwarfed the cabin, diminishing the luxurious interior into insignificance by the sheer force of his personality.

What would he be like as a lover? Tender and thought-ful, or wildly passionate, as masterful as he was sexually experienced?

Her breath came faster and, to her shock, a languorous heat flowed through her, melting her bones and setting her nerves dancing in forbidden anticipation.

What did she know about loving, about lovers? If Alex made a move she wouldn't know what to do.

He'd probably find that off-putting.

Or laughable.

Fortunately, the steward came silently through with a selection of magazines—including, she noticed, the one she wrote for.

Dragging her mind away, she checked her column, frowned at a sentence she could have framed better, then turned over a few more pages and tried to concentrate on the latest fashions.

Rassel had been right to sack her, she decided, frowning at one photograph. He was heading into punk, and she'd look ridiculous in his latest creations. She didn't suit an edgy, rebellious look—her face and persona were too conventional to cope with the wild side.

Her gaze drifted across the opulently furnished cabin to Alex, dark head bent slightly as he read his way through a mountain of papers. He must have taken a speed-reading course, she thought idly, then forced her eyes back to her magazine.

Feverishly, she pretended to examine a tall redheaded model clad in scraps of gold leather and tried to concentrate on the text beneath, but the words jerked meaninglessly in front of her eyes.

After several minutes she relaxed enough to be able to breathe easily. Her lashes drooped. The hum of the engines and last night's sleepless hours were a strong sedative. She opened her eyes and stared out the window, only to feel her skin prickle.

Was Alex watching her?

No, of course not. Disciplining herself not to glance his way, she looked down at the page again. The print blurred in front of her.

'You're tired.'

Alex's voice made her jump and the magazine slid from her lap onto the floor. She scrabbled for it but the seat belt held her fast, and helplessly she watched his lean brown hand pick the magazine up and put it down on the seat beside her.

'You might as well use the bedroom over there.' His voice was level as he nodded towards a door off the cabin. 'You'll be more comfortable there.'

Because the thought of him watching her while she slept in the seat was unbearably intimate, she nodded and unclipped her belt, only to stagger slightly when she stood up and the plane tilted a little.

Alex's eyes narrowed and his hand shot out to grip her shoulder. 'It's all right—we're crossing the mountains, and this is minor turbulence. As soon as we hit cruising altitude things will settle down.'

Automatically, Serina straightened. 'I'm not afraid, but thank you,' she said. 'I just wasn't expecting it.'

Immediately his grip loosened. 'OK now?'

'Yes. Fine.'

She headed across to the bedroom, wanting nothing more than to put some distance—and a door—between them. His touch had scrambled her brain and alerted unknown hidden pleasure points in her body, sending secret pulses of sensation through every cell.

If this uncontrollable response was desire, she not only didn't know how to deal with it, she found it down-right embarrassing.

Her breath eased out in a long jagged sigh once she'd shut the door behind her. The huge bed was opulent, the cabin decorated for sleep, relying on subtle colours and the cool play of linen against gleaming silk, the soft luxury of a caramel cashmere throw. Her gaze fixed onto the plump pillows that called to her with a siren's lure.

Yet more alluring, more compelling, was that un-bidden hunger for something she'd never experienced, something she was afraid of—the reckless, dangerously fascinating clamour of her body for a fulfilment she didn't dare seek.

'So forget about it and start behaving like a sane person,' she commanded beneath her breath.

She sat down and eased off her shoes, then swung up her legs.

But as her eyes closed she found herself wondering how many women had shared this bed with Alex.

CHAPTER THREE

THAT unwelcome query translated into Serina's dreams, darkening them with images of pursuit. She was being chased by something darkly ominous, something that intended to kill her... Although she ran until her breath came in great sobbing gasps she couldn't outpace her pursuer. A thin cry forced itself past her lips.

And then she was shaken so vigorously her teeth chattered.

'Wake up, Serina,' a deep, hard voice commanded. 'Come on, Princess, you're having a nightmare. Wake up and it will be over.'

Still in thrall to the dream, she huddled away from the imperative hand on her shoulder and catapulted towards the other side of the bed, only to be imprisoned by long fingers fettering her wrist.

Her lashes flew up; she stared at Alex Matthews' grim face and, to her horror and shock, tears burned behind her eyelids.

'It must have been a stinker,' he said harshly, his arms tightening around her so that she was hauled up into the refuge of his powerful body, her cheek against the open neck of his shirt.

Warmth enveloped her, and his faint sexy fragrance.

Gratefully, she curved into him, soaking up the bone-deep security of his vitality. She could hear his heart, fast and heavy, and anticipation burst into full flower inside her, so shameless and sudden she shuddered at the intensity of it.

Until she realised he was as aware of her as she was of him. Shocked, she jerked upwards, and this time Alex let her go.

'Oh, good lord,' she muttered, despising her lack of self-control. 'Sorry—I didn't mean to disturb you.'

And then her words registered. Heat washed her entire body in a flood of colour, and she had to stop her instinctive dive under the nearest pillow. Instead, she stared belligerently at him.

'It's all right,' he said shortly. He got to his feet and looked down at her. 'Do you have nightmares often?'

Serina managed to rally enough fragments of her usual composure to say in a voice that was almost level, 'Occasionally—but doesn't everyone?'

Not Alex Matthews, she'd be prepared to wager.

He said, 'Want to talk about it?'

'No,' she returned abruptly, then flushed. 'Sorry again; that was rude of me.'

'Sometimes talking about something will banish the fear.'

He sounded only mildly interested but after one rapid glance at him she looked away, her nerves stretched so taut she could feel them twanging.

However, he had comforted her so he deserved some sort of explanation. Reluctantly, she said, 'I think it's a standard nightmare—I was being chased, running like crazy but not being able to escape whoever or whatever was after me. I can never see what it is I'm afraid of, which is idiotic.'

If only she could see it she'd be able to face it and deal with it, but the terrifying menace had never revealed itself to her.

She should have outgrown it years ago. Her mother had told her it was a growing-up dream, a fear of leaving childhood behind and becoming an adult, but Serina no longer believed that. She'd had to grow up the year she'd turned eighteen, the year her parents had died.

'Expecting dreams to follow any sort of logic sounds like a recipe for futility,' Alex said casually.

She tried a pale smile. 'Oh, well, it's over. Thank you very much for rescuing me.'

There was no immediate answer, and she looked up again to catch a frown before he asked in the same impersonal tone, 'Can you think of any reason for having it now?'

With an attempt at her usual crispness she said, 'No. But then, as you've just pointed out, dreams don't necessarily have a reason.'

His brows smoothed out, leaving his bold face unreadable. 'A meal will be ready soon. If you'd like a shower, feel free to use the bathroom.'

'I'd like that very much.' As he turned to go, she added, 'Thank you. You've been very kind.'

'No problem,' he said over his shoulder as he left.

For a few seconds Serina sat very still, deliberately allowing her shoulders to sag while she breathed slowly and steadily in an attempt to relax.

What a fool she'd been! Dear heaven, the moment Alex lifted her she should have pulled away and found the self-control to reject his well-meant comfort politely but definitely.

Instead, she'd snuggled—yes, *snuggled*—into him as though he were her last refuge in a dangerous world.

And it had been wonderful—strong arms around her, that faint disturbing scent that was his alone, his body quickening into life against hers...

Until she'd realised what she was doing—what she'd been begging for.

Humiliation roiled through her in a sick flood. Biting her lip, she opened the door into the small, luxurious bathroom and turned the shower onto cold.

Alex looked up when she emerged, every hair in place, cosmetics subtly renewed. The mask was back, he thought sardonically, and this time set in concrete. A piercing twist of hunger took him by surprise. Irritated, he tried to banish it.

Why did she exasperate him so much? Because she'd turned a defunct royal connection into a lifestyle? A clearly profitable lifestyle, if her wardrobe was anything to go by.

No, that was unfair; her clothes were almost certainly advertisements for the designer she'd been a muse for.

What the hell did a muse do? Nothing, he suspected, beyond attracting attention and showing off the couture clothes made for her. If so, the designer had chosen well; Serina of Montevel had connections to royalty all over Europe, and she looked superb in the subtly sensuous clothes that draped her elegant body.

Which didn't alter the fact that Alex despised people who played on their heritage, their title or their position.

Yet he didn't seem to be able to despise Serina—

Princess Serina, he reminded himself. He'd not only invited her to stay with him, he'd organised a holiday for her brother to keep him out of mischief, and promised him holiday work for a year.

So why was he pushing his way into her life? Because she was a challenge?

He dismissed that thought; he'd never regarded women as trophies, the harder to win the more prestigious. As for her kid brother—well, he quite liked the boy, and keeping him away from the pack of wolves he'd inadvertently fallen in with would be to Gerd and Rosie's advantage because Montevel and Carathia shared a border.

And the Princess? She intrigued him.

Reduced to the most basic level, he wanted her. And it cut both ways—he was too experienced to misread the quick fluctuations of colour in her exquisite skin, the subtle alterations in her breathing, the tiny physical signals she couldn't control.

Fight it with everything she had—and she was certainly doing that—the elegant Princess Serina couldn't hide her response to him. Yet she'd made it plain she resented the mindless tug of desire and had no intention of acting on it. Which probably meant that just as the attraction was mutual, so was the exasperation.

It seemed a waste, but it was her decision to make.

He glanced at her serene face as she lowered herself gracefully into the chair and picked up a magazine.

Last night the woman who'd finally wrecked her parents' marriage and possibly caused their deaths had insinuated that Serina was on the lookout for a rich husband. He despised the woman—and himself for not being able to banish her words from his mind.

Perhaps Serina was saving herself for marriage, although he'd heard rumours of a couple of serious relationships. Since when had he allowed himself to worry about rumours? The elegant, intelligent, exquisitely mannered Princess with social kudos to spare would be the perfect wife for any man who could afford her.

With Gerd's marriage a sure thing, had Serina seen Rosie's half-brother—certainly not royal, but rich and well-connected—as a possible second-best?

And if Serina knew more about her brother's conspiracy than Gerd's security men had been able to uncover, then a wealthy, besotted husband would be a definite asset in their plans.

Mentally he shrugged. It wouldn't be the first time a woman had pursued him for reasons of her own, and he doubted if it would be the last. And if Princess Serina thought she could manipulate him into anything with coyness she was hugely mistaken.

He might find her very attractive, but he was fully in control of his sexual urges.

If she *had* wondered whether he was good husband material, she was clearly now having second thoughts. On that bed she'd catapulted out of his arms as though he'd been the unknown, terrifying pursuer of her dream.

Or perhaps, he thought cynically, she'd decided that giving in too soon would lower her value in his eyes…

He was surprised at his relief when the arrival of the steward offering drinks before the meal interrupted his thoughts.

After she'd eaten Serina opened her elderly laptop to map out several future columns. The previous night she'd spent some of her sleepless hours on the Internet researching New Zealand and its plant life.

'Anything I can help you with?' Alex asked casually.

'I don't know.' But he seemed interested, so she went on, 'I emailed my editor, and she's quite excited about my visit to New Zealand. Europeans know all about formal and English country gardens, but she and I are sure the readers will enjoy something different and new.'

Alex said, 'Most of the gardens will be very *in*formal, and you won't be able to give your readers a titillating glimpse into the private lives of the aristocracy. We don't have one.'

'Really?' Serina didn't try to repress her sarcasm. Was he being deliberately insulting? OK, so he had a point; on occasion she'd inserted innocuous information about the owners in her column, but she hoped that wasn't the main reason for her readers' loyalty.

'Actually,' she purred sweetly, 'if you'd ever read my column you'd know that the gardens are the stars, not the people who own them. And to make sure I haven't inadvertently invaded the owners' privacy I show them the copy before it goes to the editor.'

'So it's a collaborative enterprise?'

Repressing an unusual impulse to snap back, she returned, 'Besides, if I relied on gossip to sell my work I'd soon find my choice of gardens drying up. I've done some research, and it seems that in Northland alone there are several magnificent places that I'm sure would interest my readers.' Her smile didn't reach her eyes. 'How about yours?'

'I like it,' he said neutrally, his eyes hardening. 'But I won't allow anyone to write about it.'

'Fine,' she said, showing her teeth as she bit out the word.

Arrogant man! She hoped very much he wasn't going to be like this the whole time she was in New Zealand.

However, for the rest of the trip he was thoughtful and pleasant—and extremely stimulating, she thought gloomily as she gazed through a window at the city of Auckland sprawled out across a narrow isthmus.

She'd read, written, taken frequent walks around the cabin that eased the stiffness of the long journey, but refused to nap again in the luxurious sleeping cabin. Awash with industrial quantities of water, she was looking forward to fresh air, and a night in a bed that was firmly anchored to the ground.

She risked a glance at Alex beside her. That now familiar slow burn of sensation in the pit of her stomach made her hesitate a half-second before she said, 'It's beautiful—a splendid setting. I hadn't realised the city was so big.'

He shrugged. 'New Zealanders like living on their own land. And while we might have only four million inhabitants, a million of them live in Auckland. In area the country's almost as big as Italy.'

'How far away is Haruru?' She pronounced the word carefully.

'Well done,' he said, his smile quickening her pulse. 'It's half an hour's flight north. I'm afraid I have a function to attend in Auckland tonight, so we'll spend the night at my apartment here, then head home tomorrow morning.'

Serina thought she'd hidden her surprise, but a black

brow lifted and he said dryly, 'Perhaps I should have mentioned that before.'

Chagrined, she shook her head and made a mental memo to watch her expression more closely. 'Of course not,' she said in her most practical tone.

'I'm sorry to have to leave you alone for your first night in New Zealand.'

She laughed. 'Nonsense. The last thing I want to do is go out for the evening.'

For most of the journey he'd worked solidly, except when he joined her for meals. She'd insisted he take the bed when he decided to sleep, pointing out that as she was shorter she'd be more comfortable in the reclining chair. He'd politely accepted.

If he'd been trying to convey his total lack of interest in her, he'd succeeded.

Serina despised the pang that thought produced.

She was far too conscious of Alex to be comfortable in his presence. He made the world seem a larger, more intriguing place, stirring her senses into hyperdrive and awakening reactions—both physical and mental—that were not only inconvenient but scary.

She must have been mad to agree to come, but four weeks wasn't too long. She'd cope.

She hoped...

The plane eased down to a smooth landing at an airport near one of the city's two harbours. Customs and immigration formalities quickly over, she walked beside Alex to a waiting car.

The driver, a tall, solidly built man, olive-skinned and with finely chiselled features, greeted Alex with a smile. 'Good trip?' he asked.

Alex's return smile made him younger and more approachable than Serina had ever seen him.

'Excellent, thanks, Craig. How's the family?'

Craig beamed. 'Brilliant.' He took Serina's bag and manoeuvred it into the boot before announcing, 'The boy's walking.'

Alex laughed. 'So you don't know what's hit you?'

'He's a hell-child—into everything. It's total mayhem,' Craig told him, his proud smile contradicting his words.

Alex introduced Craig Morehu to her. They shook hands and Serina asked, 'How old is your son?'

'Ten months,' Craig said with even more pride, and grinned at her surprise. 'Yes, apparently he's advanced for his age.'

Alex said, 'Serina, if you don't mind, Craig and I need to talk business so I'll sit in the front seat with him.'

'Of course I don't mind,' she said politely, and during the journey kept her gaze to either side of the car, ignoring the width of Alex's shoulders and the incisive tone of his voice as he and the driver spoke together.

Auckland was leafy and green and busy, the motorway bordered by shrubs and trees, many of which she didn't recognise. Small volcanic cones, most covered in brilliantly green grass, seemed to pop into view wherever she looked, and the twin harbours wove in and out of the land so that each change of direction revealed a new vista.

Alex's apartment was richly welcoming, a big penthouse in a solid nineteenth-century building that had been turned into a hotel. Furnished in traditional style with huge timber-framed windows that took in magnificent views of the harbour and cityscape, the rooms were warmed by flowers.

Serina didn't know what she'd expected—something uncompromisingly minimalist to go with what she knew of Alex's character?

But the decor had probably been produced by a decorator. All Alex would have had to do was throw money at it.

Then she saw the telescope aimed at the harbour. Her father had had one just like it; it still stood in the tiny back street apartment in Nice she shared with Doran when he was home.

She repressed a swift pang of homesickness as Alex showed her into a large bedroom with its own bathroom. This was more feminine, the comfort factor still very evident.

Alex said, 'If you need anything let me know, or ring the bell. I'll be with Craig for another half an hour, and after that we could fill in time by either swimming or playing tennis on the residents' court. Which would you prefer?'

'Tennis,' she said instantly, repressing a forbidden image of him stripped down and glistening...

She suspected he was surprised, but could read nothing in his angular face as he said, 'Then tennis it will be.'

After she'd unpacked she set up her laptop and sent an email to Doran to tell him she'd arrived; he'd already sent one to her, brief but enthusiastic. Clearly, he was enjoying himself.

Spirits rising, she spent a long time in the shower, her dry skin luxuriating in the cool water. The shorts and T-shirt she changed into were neat and practical,

although when Alex saw her she was suddenly—
foolishly—too aware of her bare legs and arms.

He was wearing shorts and a shirt too, and something
very odd happened in the pit of Serina's stomach. Lean
and tanned, the lithe power of his body revealed without
the sophisticated covering of his more formal clothes,
Alex was—overwhelming.

Serina swallowed, heartily glad she'd chosen tennis.
If he had this impact on her fully clothed, she'd probably
have fainted at the sight of him in swimming trunks, she
thought disparagingly.

'What standard do you play?' he asked as they went
down to the court.

'Average. You?'

He shrugged. 'Lousy, I imagine—I haven't played for
years.'

Possibly not, but the powerful coil and flow of muscle
beneath his shirt told her he exercised in some way. And
she soon discovered he played a fierce game, revealing a
natural athleticism that forced Serina onto the defensive.
Fully extended, she set her lips firmly and fought back,
determined not to let him win easily.

As they walked back to the penthouse after her hon-
ourable defeat, he commented, 'You're a fighter.'

Was that a note of surprise in his voice? *Good*, she
thought.

'I try very hard not to lose,' she told him, conscious
of her T-shirt clinging to her damp skin and knowing
she badly needed another shower.

But she'd enjoyed the hard physical tussle, and the fact
that she'd made Alex work for his victory. One of her
mother's favourite sayings had been that a man needed

to know he was stronger than the woman in his life. Her mother had been wrong. It might apply to men who were fundamentally weak, but Serina didn't believe Alex would have been shattered if he'd been beaten. His innate self-confidence came from something much more firmly based than a constant need to prove himself a winner.

'I don't know of anyone who likes losing,' he said thoughtfully. 'I certainly don't.'

It could have been a warning, but she was oddly warmed by his considered response. It seemed to indicate a relaxation of the formidable authority she found so intimidating.

She said, 'It must be a characteristic of the men in your family. Kelt and Gerd are both win-at-all-costs men.'

'Do you think so?' He frowned. 'We like to win—we work hard at doing just that—but I wouldn't have said that any of us see victory as a goal worth achieving no matter what the cost.'

For once she'd let her tongue run away with her. 'I overstated the case,' she agreed. 'Winning is important to them, though.'

'And to the men in your family too, I understand. So do you think your brother has any chance of getting back the Montevel throne?' he asked, his tone unchanged.

Stunned, Serina stared at him. He was watching her closely, and something about his total lack of expression chilled her. She asked incredulously, 'What on earth are you talking about?'

'Come on, Princess, surely you knew your brother and a bunch of other exiled Montevellans are plotting to regain the throne?'

They had stopped at the elevator that led to the penthouse. As she stepped inside, Serina's brain came up with the answer and she started to laugh.

'You're talking about their computer game, aren't you?'

'Is that what it is?' His tone was neutral, at variance with his probing gaze, hard as quartz.

He pressed the button and the elevator whooshed upwards, leaving her stomach behind. 'How did you hear about it?' she asked.

'News gets around.'

She frowned. 'They'll be worried about that. Doran said the gaming world is really cut-throat, and they don't want anyone to know what they're working on until it's ready for production.' She looked up at Alex. 'Do you have any interests in that area?'

'No,' he said bluntly. 'And I think you've just insulted me. Even if I did have a financial interest in the creation of video games, I wouldn't steal other people's ideas.'

Serina flushed. This man had a seriously weakening effect on her normal good manners, and his reputation for integrity gave Serina no reason to disbelieve him.

Nevertheless, she asked, 'How did you get to hear about it? Doran only told *me* about it because I was angry at the amount of time he was spending on the computer, and even then he swore me to secrecy. He said they were all being really close-mouthed about it.'

'Tell me about this game,' Alex said dryly.

When she hesitated he continued with a flick of hauteur, 'Of course, if you think I can't be trusted—'

'I'm sure you can be,' Serina said, making up her mind, and rather glad to confide in someone. 'It started just before the end of last year. One of Doran's friends is an ardent game player, and apparently when they

were talking about Montevel one night he thought of
using Montevel itself, and the idea of restoring the
monarchy, as the basis for a world-building game.
They've all become fascinated by it.' Her smile was a
little lopsided. 'Partly because they hope that if it takes
off they'll become instant millionaires. Doran's had a lot
of fun working out what he'll do with his share.'

Alex lifted an eyebrow. 'And that is?'

'Sail around the world in a super yacht to all the really
good diving spots,' she told him wryly.

'So what's your part in it?'

The elevator stopped and the doors slid open. She
said, 'None—unless you count nagging Doran about
staying up all night when he's working out more tricks
and turns to the game. His latest idea is the introduction
of a nest of vampires in the mountains on the border of
Carathia and Montevel.'

Alex unlocked the door to the penthouse. Should she
tell him she was starting to get seriously concerned about
Doran's obsession with the game?

No. Loyalty to her brother and a lifetime of keeping
her own counsel warned her to stay silent.

Alex stood back to let her into the apartment. She
walked through into the living room and stopped by the
window, looking out at the view.

The sounds of the city were muted by the glass and
the wide terrace outside and, although she couldn't see
Alex, she could feel his presence behind her.

It was thanks to Alex that her brother was in
Vanuatu—and she hoped he was enjoying himself so
much that when he came back the game would no longer
have such a grip on him.

Alex said evenly, 'So it's just a fantasy war game

concocted by a group of kids brought up on stories of the good old days in Montevel?'

Serina turned. Her heart missed a beat. He was watching her mouth and a glint in the dark, unreadable blue of his eyes set her pulse skyrocketing.

'What else could it be?' Her voice shook a little, and her hands were too tightly folded—almost clenched at her sides. Deliberately, she relaxed them, producing a coolly amused smile. 'Has someone been feeding you stories of a bunch of battle-hardened revolutionaries?'

Something about Alex's answering smile—a hint of ruthlessness—sent tiny cold shivers down her spine.

But his voice was calm and reasonable. 'One of my security men heard something about their activities—but didn't realise it was a video game. Because Montevel is on Gerd's borders, he knew I'd be interested.'

'Ah, I see.' So had he offered the trip to Vanuatu—and this holiday to her—so he could find out what he wanted to know?

The suggestion had no right to hurt, but it did. She said crisply, 'Then you'll be able to reassure him—and Gerd, because I'm sure you've told him about it—that it's just a group of romantic kids play-acting rather obsessively.'

He said, 'But you're worried about it.'

Infusing her tone with a false lightness, Serina evaded, 'Irritated, actually. Doran's spending far too much time working at it—time he should be studying. I'm hoping this diving trip will give him something else to think about.'

'From the tone of your voice, I'd say you've quarrelled about it.'

He saw too much. 'I have to admit I was glad when

you suggested the trip to Doran. The time he's spending on the game is showing in his college results.' She hesitated before adding, 'I've read about young people who become addicted to video gaming...'

'*Playing* the games, not creating them,' Alex said levelly.

'That's true,' she conceded, feeling a little foolish and over-protective, 'and Doran is inclined to be very one-tracked with every new interest. It's just that this one has lasted a lot longer than any other.'

She smiled up at him. 'But, as for him and his friends being any sort of threat to Carathia or Montevel—no, they're not that far removed from reality, even if they have made grandiose plans for spending the money when they all become instant millionaires! They're all bright young men—'

'Bright young men of Montevellan descent who've been brought up with a somewhat skewed view of the country as it used to be for the upper classes before they were thrown out.'

She folded her arms. 'Did you invite Doran and me out here so you could find out more? If so, I'm afraid it's been a waste of money and time. I've no doubt that if you'd approached him while we were in Carathia for the wedding, he'd have told you all about the game.'

Alex said softly, 'Ah, but then I'd have missed the pleasure of your company.'

His words fell into a deepening pool of silence. The sounds of the city faded so that all Serina could hear was the beating of her heart.

Hurrying into speech, she said briskly, 'And no doubt that would have been a tragedy.'

'Fishing, Princess?'

Before she could answer she felt the lightest touch of his hand on her shoulder. Obeying it, she turned and looked up into a face set hard, narrowed eyes intent and crystalline.

Excitement bumped her already heavily beating heart into overdrive. Suddenly dry-mouthed, she swallowed, but words still wouldn't come. Her dilated gaze fixed on a pulse beating in his jaw, and she clenched her fist to stop herself from reaching up and touching it with a fingertip.

'Alex?' she said uncertainly.

CHAPTER FOUR

ALEX's lips barely moved when he said, 'Serina,' and traced the outline of her mouth with a lean, gentle fore-finger.

Colour burned up through her skin and her heart-beats drummed in her ears, awareness tingling through every cell and filling her with longing. Incredulously, she realised she was holding her breath, unable to summon her wits to move. Drowned in the burnished blue of his eyes, she clung single-mindedly to the simple concept of staying upright.

Then he said, 'You must know already that I'm glad you came.' And stepped away.

Serina fought to hide a fierce disappointment, keen as a knife blade. What had gone wrong? Why had he decided against...?

Against *what*, exactly?

Against kissing her.

Humiliation drove a desperate desire to gloss over the violence of her response. She said on a breath jagged enough to be painful, 'I wasn't fishing for any compliment. I was actually being slightly sarcastic.'

He hadn't answered her question so she still didn't know whether he'd invited her to New Zealand to find out what Doran and his friends were doing. Had he deliberately engineered that touch, that convincingly intense gaze, to fog her brain with sensual expectation so she wouldn't push for an answer?

If so, he knew now she wanted him more than he did her. Her response gave him power; he'd been able to pull away while she'd been frozen.

Pride came to her rescue. Stiffening her shoulders, she lifted her chin and kept her gaze level and slightly ironic. After all, it wasn't as though she'd never been kissed.

However, past kisses had been pleasant, only mildly stimulating, about as far removed as anything could be from the jolting, heady anticipation she'd experienced when Alex touched her.

What was the difference?

No other man had stirred her as Alex did, arousing a need she'd never felt before, as potent and clamorous as hunger. He was the only man able to set her hormones surging in that delicious, terrifying flood of anticipation...

Cool it, she warned her body staunchly, but she had to wait a few seconds before her voice was steady enough for her to observe in a casual tone, 'I hope you manage to convince Gerd that his concern about trouble on his borders is baseless.'

Alex's expression gave nothing away, but her skin tightened when her eyes met his, unyielding and austere.

'I'll tell him you said so,' he said, then glanced at his watch. 'I've rung the organiser of the fund-raising dinner I promised to attend tonight, and she's quite sure that if you want to come she can arrange that.'

'No, no,' she broke in. The surge of response ebbed

rapidly, leaving her lax and enervated. 'I think jet lag must have struck—I wouldn't be entertaining company tonight.'

Black brows drawn together, he scrutinised her face. 'I should have realised you'd feel the effects—I'm sorry for wearing you out at tennis.'

'You didn't,' she said promptly. 'All I need is a good night's sleep and I'll be fine.'

He nodded. 'I'll be back well before midnight. When you want to eat, use the telephone to call the restaurant and order a meal.'

Serina was relieved when he left, although the big penthouse seemed to echo emptily without his vibrant presence. After she'd eaten an excellent meal, she explored the bookshelves in a room that combined the functions of a library and media area, strangely delighted to find several well-read books she'd enjoyed too. But she couldn't settle and although she was tired enough to feel drowsy it took her a long time to get to sleep.

In fact, she didn't manage it until she heard sounds that indicated Alex had returned.

When she woke, a glance at her watch revealed she'd slept only four hours. City noises floated up to the penthouse—traffic, the distant clamour of a siren, a squeal of brakes from the street below...

Just like all other cities, she thought wearily. And, to take her mind off wondering whether Alex had really intended to kiss her, she tried to imagine what she'd hear in the countryside where he lived.

It was a lost cause. Her wilful memory kept returning to those electrifying moments when he'd touched her mouth. Dreamily, she recalled the look on his face, the charged intensity about him that had awakened her equal untrammelled response.

He *had* wanted to kiss her.

So why had he pulled back? He was experienced; she knew of at least two long-term affairs he'd had. Surely he'd read the signals clearly enough to know she wouldn't slap his face and storm out of the room?

Perhaps he'd decided it was too soon. Which was amazingly considerate of him...

And quite correct. However, there were four weeks ahead for them both to find out more about each other.

Smiling languorously, she turned over, closed her eyes and slid into sleep, waking to a morning as crisp and welcoming as a summer's day. After showering and pulling on a pair of well-cut trousers and a paler blue silk shirt that intensified the colour of her eyes, she opened the curtains and gazed out at a radiant sky beaming over the city, the harbour glinting in the sunlight and dotted with islands that danced clear and bright in the vivid sea.

On the terrace outside her bedroom window flowers bloomed in a small garden; Serina opened the door that led out onto it and on a little exclamation of surprise and pleasure bent to smell one particular potted rose, sinfully crimson with a heart as darkly potent as forbidden love.

'A rose for a rose.'

Alex's voice brought her upright so suddenly her head swam.

'Are you all right?' A second later, his hands clamped around her upper arms, 'Is there something I should know about? This must be the second or third time you've stumbled.'

Shamefully, Serina would have liked nothing more

than to rest her head on that broad chest and stay there, but an instinctive self-protection made her stiffen. 'I didn't stumble—I just missed a step each time. And I'm fine, thank you. I just straightened up too quickly.'

Alex looked down at her, a faint smile curving his mouth. For a moment Serina thought her heart stood still.

Hastily, so conscious of his hands on her skin that her thoughts dissolved under a heady burst of sensation, she finished, 'And probably a bit drunk on that gorgeous perfume. Do you know what the rose is called?'

'No, but I can find out.' He sounded abstracted, but he stepped back and when she risked an upwards glance she saw his eyes narrow, become intent and smoky. 'Did you sleep well?'

'Yes, thank you. How…how did the charity function go?'

'Very well.'

Meaningless stuff, she thought, caught in a bubble of stillness. She was babbling, and he—he wasn't concentrating on her words…

A chasm opened up in front of her. If she jumped, it would be into the unknown. She might crash—or she might find some unexplored place ablaze with possibility. Whatever, she'd never be the same again.

Much safer to stay where she was, step back, smile at him, go on talking meaningless platitudes—and leave New Zealand after four weeks, the same person she'd always been.

A coward.

Her heart began to race. Banishing fear, she lifted a hand to touch his cheek.

His smile became set, his gaze piercing. 'Sure, Princess?'

'My name is Serina,' she said, holding his eyes.

She wanted him to kiss the woman she was, not the public persona—serene princess, daughter of a long line of monarchs, scion of a defunct throne.

Serina read comprehension in his eyes, and knew that for some reason he didn't want to make the small surrender. She didn't even know why it was so important to her.

Tension sparked the silence between them, turning it heavy with desire.

'Do you know what you're asking for?' he said, a raw note altering the timbre of his voice and sending little shudders down her spine.

'Yes,' she said. 'Yes, I know. But what do *you* want?'

Something flickered in the burnished blue of his eyes and brought a half-mocking smile to that wicked mouth, with its narrow top lip buttressed by a sensuous lower one. 'A kiss,' he said. 'And I'm not asking, Serina—I'm taking what you've been silently promising me since we danced together at the wedding.'

He drew her towards him. She put a hand on his chest, looking up into an intense chiselled face. On a thrill that was half fear, half voluptuous anticipation, she thought he looked like a hunter.

Buoyed by a sudden, rather shameless relief, she nodded. Yet when he made no move she was assailed by shyness. Hot and embarrassing, colour stole along her cheekbones, but she met his eyes without wavering.

Although his eyes were still fiercely predatory, his voice became gentler. 'All right?'

'Yes.'

And when he bent his head and claimed her mouth with his own she yielded, leaning into him as he gathered her against him. White-hot sensations swamped her in a rush of adrenalin—his hard male contours, the taste of him, the faint barely-there fragrance that was his alone.

Her knees buckled and he tightened his grip, bringing her even closer to his powerful, fully aroused body.

Alex lifted his head and looked down into eyes that were slumbrous, almost dazed with passion, their violet-blue depths mysteriously dark. Gritting his teeth against a hungry surge of triumph, he fought back the primitive impulse to carry her across to the lounger a few metres away and take her then and there.

It was too soon, too public, and she deserved better than a hasty, violent consummation.

But he couldn't resist the enticement of her soft lips. When he lowered his head and claimed them again, she melted into him without resistance, her open, sensual surrender setting off a torrid chain effect that affected his every clamorous cell.

He managed to call a halt, to look into her huge eyes and say in a voice that probably sounded as taut and explosive as he felt, 'Serina—we have to stop this right now or it will be too late.'

Her lashes fell slowly, trembled against skin as translucent as the finest silk, but when she lifted them again she was once more in command of herself.

'So we stop,' she said, a husky note in her voice giving her away.

Alex found himself wishing he'd taken the chance. For the first time ever he'd lost control, been tempted to follow his desires and damn the consequences.

Mastering his hunger, he released her and tried to summon his usual detached attitude. The aftermath of a carnal storm unlike anything he'd ever experienced made it near impossible.

Who'd have thought the gracious, reserved Princess would show all the instincts of a courtesan?

No, most courtesans had their eyes firmly on their bank balances, bargaining sex for security. Serina had offered herself ardently and without reserve.

And then he wondered whether she'd have been so passionately willing if they hadn't spoken about her brother.

Even as the thought formulated, he knew it wasn't likely. She seemed convinced that Doran and his friends were designing a video game, so why would she be concerned? She also guessed he'd warned Gerd about the possibility of trouble on his borders.

However, he had to assume that she might have been lying. An inner revulsion at the thought forced him to realise how much he wanted to trust her. The computer game story was a brilliant subterfuge, entirely believable. Pity it wasn't true. Young Doran and his band of romantic, eager conspirators had no idea what they'd got into.

He looked down into her face and saw with savage satisfaction that she too was struggling for control. The ache in his groin intensified into a plea, a demand—almost a command. He fought it back because he didn't dare give his innermost instinct free rein.

He'd be betraying Gerd and Rosie if he didn't make every effort to find out whether Serina knew anything—any small scrap of information that could lead them to the people who were backing her brother and his friends.

In spite of their efforts, he and Gerd still weren't sure who was pulling the strings, or why, although they had their suspicions. If the Princess had any inkling, he was honour bound to find out.

And if that meant seducing her into pillow talk, then it would have to be done. It was, quite literally, a matter of life and death, not only for her brother and his friends, but for many other people.

Serina looked up, catching a glimpse of something harsh and grim in his eyes. Chilled, she masked a shiver by turning away so she could pretend to examine the rose again.

'I'm sorry,' he said evenly.

'Why?' She even managed a smile. 'I know the tabloids call me the ice princess, but surely you don't believe them? I have been kissed before.'

His brows rose and he surprised her by stooping to snap off the bloom and hold it out to her. In a wry voice he told her, 'I'm sorry because I stupidly made the arrangement for our flights without thinking that we might want to prolong our stay here.'

Colour heated her skin. Now—or *never,* she thought, wondering if he could hear her heart thudding so heavily in her chest.

Now. Because she wanted to know what making love to Alex was like infinitely more than she wanted to obey the strictures drummed into her by her mother and her governess. For the first time in her life she realised how potent desire could be...

'I—thank you,' she said, and answered his unspoken proposition by lifting the flower to her lips, still tender from his kisses. The petals were warm and smooth and she inhaled their sweetly provocative perfume.

Hastily, she said, 'I don't think I've ever seen a rose exactly this shade of red before. And, as it seems perfectly happy growing in a pot, I'd like to buy one for myself when I get back home. It should enjoy living on my balcony, and it would be a charming reminder of my visit here.'

'If you want a true reminder of New Zealand, a native plant might be more appropriate. You can buy sealed packets of seeds that are acceptable to most countries now.'

How could he switch so abruptly—from the passionately demanding kisses of a few minutes ago to this pleasant, conversational courtesy?

With ease, clearly. Emotion and sensation were still churning through her, but Alex was once more fully in control.

'I'll look out for them.' She turned to go, but remembered something. 'What time do you plan to leave this morning?'

He paused, as though remembering something. 'There's been a change of plan—if you're happy with it. I met friends at the dinner last night who live not far north of here in a vineyard. Their garden is beautiful—a showpiece. Today they're launching their latest red with lunch and a reception there. They invited me and, when I mentioned you were with me, they extended the invitation to you.'

'That's very kind of them,' she said uncertainly.

His brows lifted. 'How is it that in your conversation I so often hear a *but* coming?'

The ironic question brought a smile. 'I'd love to meet them, and the launching of a new wine is a very special occasion…'

Her voice trailed away. How could she explain that she didn't want to appear to his friends as his latest conquest, arm candy for a successful man?

Before she could go any further, he said, 'New Zealanders are notoriously informal, and I can promise you the invitation is genuine. Aura suggested we come for lunch and look around their garden as that's your interest.' And, when she hesitated anew, he added, 'She recognised your name and has read some of your columns.'

Somehow that appeased her uncertainty. 'I'd love to go,' she said quietly.

He glanced at his watch. 'Then we'd better move. Breakfast will be in about twenty minutes.'

'I'll be there,' she promised and headed back into her bedroom.

Once inside, she stood still in the middle of the room and took several deep breaths, trying to clear the fog of confusion and frustrated desire from her brain.

The perfume from the rose drifted up, softly seductive, and she said beneath her breath, 'That's enough of that, thank you! I need a clear head right now.'

She filled a glass with water and popped the flower into it, ruefully examining a tiny bead of bright blood where a thorn had broken the skin on her thumb.

For some reason she didn't want to analyse what had happened out there on the terrace. Tiny tantalising prickles of sensation ran across her skin as she remembered...

Stop it, she commanded her wayward mind. So she enjoyed Alex's kisses—too much—and, judging by his initial reaction, he'd enjoyed her response.

And then he'd shut down. Again.

Why? And where—if anywhere—did they go from here?

She stared at the mirror, absently taking in the luxurious cream and gold opulence of the bathroom. Very feminine. And she'd better not forget that other women would have used this room.

The thought tarnished the residual excitement of his kisses, her pleasure in the day, in the rose.

Once she'd been the unwilling witness to a scene between her mother and her father, when her father had said impatiently, 'It means nothing, my dear. You are and will always be the only woman I love—any others are mere entertainment.'

Her mother had asked wearily, 'Do all men feel that way?'

And her father, probably made uncomfortable by his wife's unspoken grief, had blustered a little before replying, 'Yes. All the ones I have met, anyway. It is simply the way men are.'

Serina's experience had backed up her father's words. Many men—and women—didn't need to love, or even *like* someone to want them.

Serina knew she wasn't that sort of person. She'd promised herself that she'd wait for someone special, someone who would make her feel things she'd never felt before, someone she could respect...

And a year ago that imaginary *someone* became concrete when she'd met Alex. Now she understood that her wildfire physical response to him had made that decision, rather than anything she knew of his character. In danger of letting passion override everything else, she needed to be absolutely sure of her feelings. And to do that she'd have to learn more about him, respond to him intellectually and emotionally as well as with this consuming, elemental hunger.

Only then could she take the next step.

And by then, she thought with an inward quiver of excitement, she'd understand what that next step should be.

In the meantime, she'd better work out what she should wear to a lunch and reception to launch a new wine.

She chose a sleek, sophisticated suit of fine wool in a deep crimson.

When she emerged in it Alex looked at her and asked, 'Did you choose that to match the colour of the wine?'

'It never occurred to me,' she said, half-laughing.

They drove to the vineyard, where his friends made her welcome. The Jansens were a few years older than Alex, and they lived with their four children in a magnificent house overlooking a wide valley braided with vines that ran down to an estuary. They were a striking couple, interesting and informative, and their garden was superb, a blend of native plants and subtropical exotica that transfixed Serina.

The guests at the launch were an equally international selection; Serina enjoyed chatting with the local residents, and was delighted to see an old friend, daughter of the royal house in a Mediterranean island, now living in a vineyard in the South Island with her handsome husband.

There were others she recognised too. As she sipped an exquisite champagne-style wine at the reception, she caught the eye of another old friend making his way towards them. The handsome scion of a famous French champagne house, Gilberte swooped on her, kissing her on both cheeks.

'Dearest Serina,' he said extravagantly, 'what on earth are you doing here in the uttermost ends of the earth?'

'She's with me,' Alex said from behind her.

Smile widening, Gilberte looked up. 'Ah, Alex, I should have known you'd be with the most beautiful woman here—apart from our hostess, of course!'

Serina laughed. 'Same old Gilberte—a compliment for every woman,' she said affectionately, aware of a prickle of tension that had nothing to do with Gilberte. 'What are *you* doing in the den of the opposition?'

'Oh, Flint and I are old friends,' he told her, 'and I come often to New Zealand—just to keep a watch on what they are doing, you understand, but also because I love the place. And because we still sell a lot of champagne here.'

Later, she looked from the window of the small commercial aeroplane as they flew the length of the long, narrow spine of Northland.

Beside her, Alex said, 'Admit it—you were surprised by the people you met at Flint and Aura's launch.'

'A little,' she admitted reluctantly. 'Because New Zealand is so far from anywhere—and looks so small on the map, lost in a waste of ocean—I suppose I'd expected a very insular group, although I'd heard that New Zealanders are extremely friendly.'

'Well-travelled too,' he drawled. 'And accustomed to overseas visitors—we get a lot of them.'

She flashed him a rueful smile. 'All right, I will admit that the very cosmopolitan guests at the launch surprised me. Apart from the lovely people, the whole occasion was like something out of a dream—the valley with vines braiding the hills and the lovely glimpse of sea, that beautiful house and the wonderful gardens, and some truly fabulous clothes.'

'I'd have thought you were accustomed to occasions like that,' Alex observed, his tone ambiguous.

'It was—' Serina stopped herself from finishing with *special*. Because, although she'd thoroughly enjoyed the occasion, it had been made special by Alex. She ended lamely, '—lovely. So friendly and warm and—well, just plain fun! The setting was exquisite. I liked your friends very much, and the wine they produce is an inspiration.'

Alex said, 'I asked Aura and Flint if you could feature their garden.'

'I—thank you so much,' she said, more than a little surprised, and touched too. Because they were his friends, she hadn't ventured anywhere near that subject. 'That was very kind of you.'

He said, 'They're happy for you to do that, but not immediately—it's holidays next week so they're taking the children to the Maldives. When they come back they'll get in touch and we'll go down in the helicopter.'

'You have a helicopter?'

'I share one with Kelt, who lives not far away.'

Well, what had she expected? He shared a private jet with Kelt and Gerd, and as a businessman with worldwide interests he'd need to travel a lot.

She turned her head to scan the two separate seas that gleamed on either side of a green land folded into hills and valleys.

'The Pacific Ocean on the right,' Alex told her, pointing out an island-studded coast where beaches gleamed golden and white. He indicated the other side. 'And the Tasman Sea on the left.'

The Tasman coast was wilder, more rugged, with no islands and long stretches of cliff-bound shore. Rows of breakers marched onto black glistening beaches that swept for miles. Between the seas were farmlands, small villages, the dark sombreness of vast tracts of pine plantations, and mountains covered in a dense cloak of trees.

'It might look pristine and untouched, but most of it was milled for kauri during the nineteenth century,' Alex said when she remarked on the huge areas of forest. 'Originally this was a land of bush, insects and birds, many of them flightless. The only mammals here were three species of bats, plus the seals and sea lions and dolphins and orca and whales in the seas around the coast.'

She said wistfully, 'It must have been breathtaking to be the first person to step on its shores.'

He regarded her with a slight smile. 'An explorer at heart, Serina?'

'Not until now,' she said, wondering if he might read the underlying meaning in the words.

If he did, he didn't respond. 'The Maori colonised New Zealand from tropical islands. They brought kiore—Maori rats—and dogs that started the destruction of the native wildlife, and of course fire and stone axes travelled with them as well. Yet, even after eight hundred or more years of occupation, the birdlife was enough to make the first Europeans marvel at the dawn chorus. Apparently it was so loud they could hardly hear each other speak.'

He pointed out a swathe of silvery trees marching

across hills by the sea. 'Olives—a very successful crop here. And those darker trees are avocados.' He settled back in his seat. 'More predators arrived with the European colonists. Apart from a few visionaries well ahead of their time, people have only recently realised how much has been lost, and started working to bring back some of the glories of the past.'

Fascinated, Serina asked, 'How are they doing that?'

He lifted a brow. 'If you're really interested, I'll take you to see something I'm connected with.'

His sceptical tone irritated her. Did he think she was foolish enough to pretend an interest just to match his?

Probably, she thought realistically.

And why not? He was rich, well-connected and hand-some—and, even more than that potent package deal, he possessed a charismatic presence, his combination of effortless male sexuality and compelling authority making him stand out in any company. He probably had gorgeous women flinging themselves at him all the time, wide-eyed with anticipation.

Like several at the launch that afternoon...

The smile she gave him was cool with an edge. 'Oh, I couldn't think of taking up your valuable time,' she said sweetly. 'If you give me a map, I'll check it out.'

'No,' he said calmly. 'It's on my land. I'll take you. We've predator-fenced an area of bush, and when we've trapped the rats and weasels and possums and feral cats inside, we'll return some of the birds that no longer live there.'

Her mother had always said the way to interest a man was to let him talk about himself. Deliberately ignoring the maternal instructions, Serina said, 'I'd love to see it. What's the name of that town beneath us?'

'Whangarei,' he said. 'Northland's only city.'

She looked down. 'It has a glorious setting—those amazing mountains reaching out into the coast, and the harbour curling up into the heart of the town. But then, everything I've seen so far is breathtaking.'

'There are ugly parts too, of course,' he said judicially. 'Some of our towns are old and tired, and some have been built with no regard for the countryside that surrounds them.'

Clearly he loved this part of New Zealand. She said, 'I've read and heard quite a bit about the South Island, but not very much at all about the north.'

'The South Island is magnificent; we'll see whether we can get you there before you go back. But I was born and bred in the north—it's always been home, so to me it's the most beautiful place in the world.'

Without thinking, she said, 'It must be wonderful to feel that way about a place.'

'You don't?'

'No,' she said, wishing she'd stayed silent. 'My parents were Montevellan, and they continually longed to go back. Nice—the Riviera—was only ever a temporary base for them. I think I was born homesick for a place I've never known. I've always felt alien.' She shook her head, meeting hooded blue eyes with a tingle of sensation. 'No, alien is too strong a word; dislocated would be better.'

'You speak English like a native,' he commented idly.

She shrugged. 'Doran and I shared an English nanny

and then a governess from Scotland until I went away to school.'

He didn't seem overly interested—and why should he be? But he asked, 'You've not been to Montevel?'

'We can't go. The government banned any member of the royal family from returning.'

'Ever felt like taking another identity and slipping in to find out what it's like? Seeing it might wipe out that inborn nostalgia; few places live up to the praise of the people who love them.'

'I've got the same face as my grandmother,' she said dryly. 'I don't think I'd get in. Anyway, I don't have the courage—or feel the need so badly that I'd break the law to do it.'

'Does your brother feel the same way?'

Alex watched the expression flee from her face; not a muscle moved, but he felt her resistance as palpably as though she'd shouted it at him.

'I think so,' she said remotely, turning her head so that he couldn't see her face.

He settled back into his seat. Whether or not she knew about Doran's plotting, she was worried about him. Which probably—no, *possibly*, Alex corrected himself—meant she did know. Perhaps, in spite of her apparent resignation to her fate, she did crave being a princess of Montevel, in fact as well as in title. He toyed with the idea of asking her directly, but decided against it.

She turned back, and his gut tightened in spontaneous homage. However hard he tried to rationalise his reaction to Serina—and he'd tried damned hard for a fair amount of the previous night—the moment her fingertips had caressed his cheek, such hunger had clamoured through him that he'd forgotten all those excellent reasons for not getting too emotionally involved with her.

Kissing her had been a revelation.

And watching young Gilberte kiss her cheeks had been like a call to arms, a primitive response that negated his understanding that it was nothing more than a greeting between friends. For a moment he'd had to rein in an urge to knock the man away from Serina.

His body clenched. Ruthlessly, he pushed the memory to the back of his mind. Gerd needed information—information he wouldn't get if Alex let his rampant hormones fog his usually logical mind.

Had Serina decided to deflect his interest by pretending to be interested in him?

Two, he thought succinctly, could play at that game.

And if he hurt her?

She might be hurt, he conceded, hardening his resolve, but if her brother went ahead with his plans she'd grieve infinitely more, because it was highly unlikely Doran would survive a foray into Montevel.

Alex made up his mind.

CHAPTER FIVE

THE plane began to descend. Serina swallowed, looking down at a large valley with two small rivers winding through it. They joined to make a lake-like estuary separated from the sea by a gold and amber sandbank. Green and lush, the valley looked remote, like some enchanted place cut off from the rest of the world.

Intrigued, she leaned forward and watched the ground rush to meet them as they banked over another range of hills towards a small airfield. Several private planes were lined up outside a hangar, and she noted two helicopters to one side, as well as a quite large parking area outside another building.

Not exactly the back of beyond, as her nanny used to say.

From beside her, Alex said, 'Ohinga,' pointing to a coastal village tucked away beside another, much bigger river, its banks lined with trees. 'Our nearest shopping centre.'

Catching the shimmer of water beneath foliage, Serina said in surprise, 'Those trees seem to be growing in the water.'

'They're mangroves. They prefer brackish water like tidal rivers and estuaries.'

Mangroves? Serina digested this as the engines changed pitch and they slanted down towards the runway. The excitement she'd been controlling ever since she arrived in New Zealand began to bubble, mixed with a trace of apprehension.

It was sheer overheated fantasy to feel that Alex's searing kisses had pushed her into unknown territory and changed her life for ever. She wasn't the sort of person such dramatic, unlikely experiences happened to—and they were only kisses, for heaven's sake. Not exactly a novelty!

But if his kisses could do that, what would she feel if he touched her even more intimately?

Heat suffused her as her body reacted to that highly subversive thought with brazen excitement.

Even with her eyes fixed onto the scene below, she could sense him beside her—as though he'd imprinted on her at some cellular level, made an indelible impression she'd never be rid of, for ever a part of her...

Oh, calm down and stop being an idiot, she told herself trenchantly. He's very sexy, very sure of himself, very experienced and he kisses like a god, but he's just a man.

Once they were safely down she swallowed hard, cast a glance his way and managed to say staidly, 'I thought mangroves were tropical trees.'

'They are, but New Zealand has the furthermost south of all mangroves. They grow along estuaries in the northern half of the North Island.'

'I wonder how they got here?' Mangroves were safe. If she concentrated on them she wouldn't be tempted to allow her eyes to linger on his formidably masculine features. 'I know the seeds float, but there's a lot of sea between here and the tropics.'

He smiled. Serina's treacherous heart somersaulted.

'One suggestion is that seeds could have drifted across from Australia, but I believe the latest theory is that New Zealand and New Caledonia were once connected by a ridge of land or possibly a chain of islands, so the mangroves could have island-hopped south.'

Serina wrinkled her brow, feverishly trying to recollect where New Caledonia was.

'A large island well to the north and west of us,' Alex provided helpfully.

She nodded as the mental image of the map clicked into place. 'Colonised by France?'

'Yes, and still proudly French.'

Don't look at him—think trees. 'So the mangroves would have had to adapt to a colder climate here?'

'Unless they came south during a warmer era and adapted as it slowly got cooler.'

'Fascinating.' But she couldn't think of anything further to say about mangroves. Now what? she thought desperately.

His expression revealed a certain wry amusement. 'I doubt if many people other than botanists would agree.'

That made her sound like some nerd.

Fortunately, the pilot announced their arrival and everyone stood, the bustle of disembarking saving her the necessity of having to reply.

OK, so nerd she was. That had to be an advance on considering her just another effete aristocrat trading on a title to earn a living.

Anyway, she thought stoutly, I don't care what he thinks. And knew she lied.

Again, a car was waiting for them on the ground but, instead of a well-dressed businessman, this driver was a woman a few years older than Serina, clad in jeans and a woollen jersey that didn't hide any of her admirable assets.

'Hi, Alex,' she greeted him cheerfully. 'Good trip?'

To Serina's surprise, Alex bent his head and dropped a swift kiss on her cheek before saying, 'Serina, this is Lindy Harcourt, who manages Haruru's finances for me. Lindy, Princess Serina of Montevel.'

'Just Serina, thank you,' Serina emphasised, and held out her hand. 'How do you do, Lindy.'

Lindy's grip was strong. 'Oh, good, I was wondering if I'd have to call you Your Highness.'

'Not if you want me to answer,' Serina said forthrightly.

The other woman bestowed a smile on Serina that held no more than a hint of speculation. 'That's all right, then.' She glanced down at Serina's suitcase. Clearly she'd expected more because she commented, 'I needn't have brought the Land Rover, after all.'

Which made a foolishly sensitive Serina wonder if Alex's female visitors usually arrived with a vast wardrobe. Assuming she'd have no need for them, she'd sent most of her formal clothes back to Nice.

Too late now, she decided pragmatically, shrugging off the thought.

Alex picked up his and Serina's bag and headed through the small arrivals area. She was intrigued when various people there nodded to him; clearly he was liked, but an element of respect in their attitudes impressed her. These people, like the guests at the wine launch, instinctively recognised his formidable strength.

Out in the car park, Alex said to Lindy, 'The keys, please.'

'Oh, sorry.' She handed them over and once the vehicle was unlocked slipped into the back seat.

Alex swung the bags into the boot, then held open the door to the front passenger seat and Serina got in, wondering about Lindy Harcourt. There was an easy camaraderie about her interaction with Alex that spoke of something more than simple friendship.

To her shock, Serina realised she was prickly as a cat, tense and smouldering with a completely unrealistic jealousy. The kisses they'd exchanged didn't give her any claim on Alex.

As he set the Land Rover into motion Lindy leaned forward and asked, 'So how did Rosie's wedding go?'

'Very well,' Alex said briefly.

Lindy's laugh held a note of amused resignation that should have soothed Serina's feelings. 'And that's all you're going to say about it, I suppose. Serina, you'll have to tell me everything.'

'I'd be glad to,' Serina said. She added, 'I don't think I've ever seen anyone look so completely happy.'

'Rosie does radiance very well,' Lindy said.

Serina bristled. It seemed an odd thing to say in front of Rosie's brother. 'She looked utterly exquisite and yes, very happy, but I was actually referring to Gerd. They made a magnificent couple.'

Surely that would put an end to any conjecture about whether or not her heart was broken. Almost certainly she was being absurdly—and uncharacteristically—over-sensitive; nobody here could possibly be interested in gossip from half the world away!

Her eyes drifted to Alex's hands, lean and competent on the wheel as he manoeuvred the Land Rover onto the road. Adrenalin tore through her, clouding her brain and fuelling a nerve-racking increase in heart rate.

She twisted to look out of the side window. How could a glimpse of his hands do that? It was almost indecent.

Valiantly, she kept her eyes fixed on the countryside sliding past them—lush green pastures backed by ranges tinged a soft silver-blue as they disappeared into the distance.

Trees, she thought, remembering the mangroves.

She swallowed and said briskly, 'What are those trees? The ones so shamelessly flaunting their autumn leaves? I didn't expect autumn colour here—I had the impression the climate was almost subtropical.'

'Not quite—warm temperate is the official classification,' Alex told her, turning off the bitumen onto a narrow road that immediately began to twist its way up into the hills. 'Which means we can ripen certain sorts of bananas here. The liquid ambers you noticed are some of the few that do colour up in the north, along with persimmons and Japanese maples.'

From the back Lindy asked, 'Are you interested in gardening, Serina?'

'Very,' Serina told her.

'The Princess writes a column for one of the European glossies,' Alex said. He sent a sideways glance at Serina. 'Although it's more about gardens than gardening, I assume.'

Keeping her voice cool, she said, 'Yes.'

Lindy said, 'Then you'll love staying with Alex. His garden is magnificent.'

'I'm looking forward to seeing it,' Serina responded.

The narrow road became a drive, winding down a hill through vast trees. Noting a fantastic oak that would have been several hundred years old in Europe, she realised that northern hemisphere trees must grow much more rapidly in Northland.

And Lindy was absolutely correct—they were magnificent. A great buttressed mound of foliage caught her attention and she twisted in her seat as they passed by it.

'A Moreton Bay fig from Queensland in Australia,' Alex told her. He slanted a glance her way. 'Unfortunately, the fruit isn't edible.'

'Sad,' she returned lightly. 'I love figs. Oh!'

She leaned forward to examine a clump of jade-green trees that turned into one massive tree.

'Puriri,' Alex said. 'They're actually a bush tree, but they don't seem to mind living in paddocks.'

'If they were any happier they might take over the country,' Serina said, amusement colouring her tone.

And then they drove through a grove of different trees and up to a house set in a great sweep of lawns. 'Oh,' Serina breathed on a long exhalation.

Alex's home was glorious. He stopped the vehicle in a gravelled forecourt and, while Serina was still gazing at the long façade of the big house, Lindy came round and opened the front passenger door for her.

Feeling awkward, Serina said, 'Thank you,' and stepped out onto the gravel.

Alex collected the bags from the boot. Putting them

on the gravel, he said, 'Thank you, Lindy—I'll see you later.'

Lindy's smile remained firmly in place, but a certain stiffness about the set of her shoulders made Serina wonder again at their relationship.

'No problems,' the other woman said cheerfully. She bestowed that determined smile on Serina. 'I'm sure you'll enjoy your stay here.'

Once she was out of earshot, Alex said, 'Welcome to my home, Serina.'

'It's amazing,' she told him. 'I don't think I've ever seen anything like it.' His friends lived in a sophisticated modern house—Alex's home was clearly a relic of the colonial period.

'High Victoriana,' he explained easily. 'It was built in the late nineteenth century for an Anglo-Indian who exported horses from here to India. Verandas were fashionable then, and he rather went overboard on them.' He bent to pick up their bags.

'I can carry mine,' Serina said, reaching for it. Their hands collided and she jerked back.

Alex straightened with both bags. Eyes gleaming, he said, 'My touch isn't poisonous.'

'I know that,' she blurted, for once unable to think straight. She added, 'Neither is mine.'

They measured glances for a moment and reckless excitement welled up inside her in a warm, heady flood.

Alex said deliberately, 'Lindy is the daughter of the woman who used to be our housekeeper. She's dead now, but Lindy and I more or less grew up together until I was sent away to school. In many ways she's as much of a sister to me as Rosie.'

He was telling her that Lindy meant nothing to him—well, nothing emotional, Serina amended.

Actually, he probably meant nothing emotional in a sexual way, because he was clearly fond of the other woman.

In spite of her efforts, Serina found she couldn't be adult and sophisticated about Alex and the way she felt. The sensations coursing through her suffered a far-from-subtle transmutation into a rising tide of anticipation.

Trying to quell it, she asked, 'How old were you then?'

'Seven.' He headed up the steps and onto the stone-floored veranda.

Horrified, Serina followed. She'd heard of small English children being sent off to school, but she had no idea New Zealanders did the same. Before she could formulate some meaningless comment, Alex looked down at her.

'After my mother died, my father married again. His new wife found a noisy, grubby, resentful child too much to handle, so off I went to school. Which is why Rosie and I have a rather distant relationship for siblings—we only spent time together in the holidays.'

Serina ached for the child he'd been, a small boy sent away from the only home he'd known, away from his playmates, from his father and the housekeeper—and the little sister—who'd been the only constants in his life.

She said, 'I'm so glad my parents waited until Doran and I were in our teens before they banished us to school.'

He opened the front door. 'I think Rosie had the worst of it. I settled into school quite well, but when Rosie was born her mother discovered she was no more maternal with her than she had been with me. And since my father, an archaeologist, was rarely here, Lindy's mother was the only reliable motherly figure Rosie ever really had. And then she died when Rosie was eight.'

Serina's heart was touched anew. Her parents' marriage hadn't been a comfortable one, but at least they'd been there for her and Doran. 'I had no idea. Still, she's got Gerd now, and I can tell he adores her just as much as she loves him.'

She wondered then if Alex might think she was hinting about being someone like that for him. Nonsense, she thought stoutly. You're being ridiculous again!

Alex said calmly, 'Yes, I believe they'll make each other happy.'

The wide, high-ceilinged hall was superbly furnished with antiques, mostly English from the Georgian period. A superb wooden staircase, exquisitely carved in some golden wood, wound its way up to another floor.

'Your bedroom is here,' Alex said once they'd climbed it, and opened a door, standing back to let her go in.

The room was big and airy, dominated by a wide bed. French windows led out onto another wide veranda; beneath and beyond it stretched lawns and a haze of flowers and palms against a background of those splendid trees.

After a quick glance around, Serina smiled. 'I can see why you decided on this room for me. You're determined to make sure I learn something about New Zealand's plants, aren't you?'

'My grandmother was a botanical artist,' he told her as she walked across to examine a series of exquisite watercolours. 'These are some of hers.'

'She was an exceptionally good one,' Serina said seriously. She peered at the signature, and said in a hushed voice, 'Oh—*Freda Matthews!* She's acknowledged as one of the greatest botanical artists of the twentieth century. And she's your grandmother!'

It was foolish to feel that somehow this forged a fragile link between them, but she couldn't hide the pleasure that the slight connection gave her.

'She died before I was born so I never knew her.' He dropped her bag onto a low stool.

'She left a superb legacy,' Serina said earnestly, examining each image with intent appreciation.

'Thank you. I think.'

His voice was grave but a note in it caught her attention. She turned her head, caught a betraying glint of amusement in his eyes and laughed up at him, her tension easing. 'Oh, you and Rosie as well, of course!'

'There's that little catch of laughter again. Do you know how infectious it is?'

Something had happened—an unspoken exchange of potent meaning that drove every trace of amusement from her.

And from Alex.

A heady awareness sizzled between them, blocking the breath in her throat. Serina's eyes widened endlessly as he came towards her with the lithe, purposeful gait of a hunter.

Almost silently, he said, 'It's also very, very sexy. And when you look over your shoulder there's something—I don't even know what it is, but you look fey.' His voice deepened. 'And maddeningly irresistible.'

Serina swallowed to ease her suddenly dry mouth.

Part of her wanted desperately to defuse the situation, to let him know that she didn't…wasn't yet ready…

And then he turned her to face him, and she looked up mutely into a face drawn and arrogant with desire. Her instinctive, protective resistance crumbled under the impact of a hunger so consuming she sighed as he fitted her into his arms and kissed her.

At first he didn't give her the passion she craved; his mouth touched hers gently, almost tenderly, so that she wanted to stand on tiptoe and *insist* he satisfy the need he'd roused in her.

Yet a slow, languorous heat melted her bones until she could do nothing but accept that silky caress.

Against her lips, he said, 'Is this what you want, Serina?'

'You know it is,' she whispered, unable to temporise, to hedge, even though some distant area of her brain was struggling to send out an All Systems alert.

He gathered her more closely into him, his mouth crushing down on hers in a kiss so ruthlessly demanding her knees almost gave way. And then she wasn't aware of anything but the wild reaction of her eager body, a surrender that overrode every sensible limit she'd lived by until then.

When at last he lifted his mouth, Serina realised he was every bit as aroused as she was. She thrilled to the harsh indrawn breath he took and the urgent lift of his chest, the tense flexion of his arms around her.

And the hard, leashed power of him against her hips.

Yet, despite all the turmoil of thwarted passion, she'd never felt so safe, so wonderfully secure.

And that was the danger, she thought, confusion

tumbling around her brain as her breathing slowed into harmony and his arms relaxed.

'Serina,' he said quietly, resting his cheek against her forehead. 'That will have to be enough for now.'

A chill shuddered through her, and she had to stifle a small sound of protest. As though he understood how shaken she still was, he held her for several seconds more until she was able to straighten and trust her knees enough to pull away.

She could read nothing in his face; the dense, crystalline blue of his gaze hid his thoughts, his emotions.

Words falling into the stiff silence like pebbles in a pond, she said through slightly swollen lips, 'I'm going to be crass and ask why.'

Alex's twisted smile held more ruefulness than amusement. 'Because it's almost dinner time, and my housekeeper will wonder what the hell we're doing if we don't arrive for it.'

Her laughter sounded almost like a sob. Hastily, she controlled it, veiling her turbulent gaze with her lashes while she tried to sort out what she wanted to say.

Alex finished, 'And because you're not ready.' He paused. 'A year ago we looked at each other and wanted each other, but the time wasn't right. I don't know if it is yet. I sense some sort of restraint in you.'

His tone was neutral, but his keen scrutiny unnerved her. Not restraint—no, not that. What he sensed was shyness, the modesty of a woman who was still a virgin.

Should she tell him? No.

She bit her lip. 'I didn't come here hoping for—*intending*—any sort of—of…' Her voice trailed away.

'Relationship? I despise that word.' His tone was cool,

almost mocking. 'Affair? Not much better. What exactly did you come here not expecting?'

Serina's brows lifted and she said with a cutting edge to each word, 'I don't like *relationship* either, but it will suffice.'

She stopped because she didn't know what to say next.

He was silent, his face expressionless, and then to her shock he linked his fingers around her wrist so that his thumb rested on the vulnerable pulse that beat there.

Sheer astonishment held her frozen, but to her dismay she felt the answering leap of her heart at that almost casual grip.

'Whatever you hoped or intended or resisted,' he said, holding her eyes with his own, 'your response tells me—and should convince you, however much you'd like to deny it—there already *is* a relationship.' He emphasised the word enough to lift the hairs on the back of her neck.

'I don't—'

Alex cut in ruthlessly, 'What you decide to do about it is up to you, but don't deny it's there.' He released her. 'And you're not in any danger. I can control my urges, and I'm sure you can too.'

His detached tone and ironic eyes set a barrier between them that hurt when it should have reassured.

After a glance at his watch he said, 'Dinner will be ready soon. I'll come and collect you in about twenty minutes.'

Once he'd left, the memory of the kiss hung in the room like the rose she'd packed so carefully—so foolishly—in her luggage. She opened her bag and picked up the bloom, limp and already fading in the tissue she'd wrapped around it, and made to throw it into the rubbish bin.

But something stayed her hand. Smiling wanly at her weakness, she put it back into the case.

'A shower,' she told herself.

As though she could wash away the memory of their kisses! She had a feeling they'd stay with her all her life—the first time she'd discovered such a depth of passion in herself that she literally had no control over her emotions.

The en suite bathroom was small but superbly fitted, and again she wondered how many women had been accommodated in this room, this house—in Alex's arms.

He certainly wasn't considered a playboy but, apart from Ms Antonides, his name had been linked with several other women, all beauties, and mostly women with high-flying careers in various fields.

About as far removed from her as anyone could be, Serina thought, turning off the water with a vicious twist of her wrist.

Then she shook her head. OK, so she didn't have a proper career, but she'd had to put any hopes of that on hold when her parents had been killed. Left with an estate that was a total mess, she'd salvaged what she could, ruthlessly selling everything of any value so Doran could finish his education at his expensive school. And becoming Rassel's muse—backed by years of serious scrimping—had provided her with enough to pay for his university studies.

Which was why she found his near-obsession with that game so infuriating. Once, when she'd taxed him with it, he'd told that one day he'd be looking after her and, although she was touched, she tried to convince him that it wasn't likely. Some research on video gaming had convinced her it was big companies who came up with profitable new franchises, not rank amateurs.

But Doran was clearly having a fabulous time in Vanuatu, so she could stop worrying about him. For the moment, anyway.

She paced around the room, admiring the delicate, exquisitely precise watercolours on the walls. Alex's grandmother had had huge talent, and her heart warmed at this further evidence of his thoughtfulness.

Her gaze drifted to the laptop. After dinner she'd make notes about what she'd seen so far while the memories were fresh.

Her heart raced when someone tapped on her door. Bracing herself, she opened it and found Alex, his expression coolly non-committal as he gave her a swift glance that encompassed her bare arms and throat.

'You might want a wrap or a cardigan.'

'I'll get one,' she said, wishing she'd thought of it herself. That impersonal survey had hurt a vulnerable part of her she'd never known she possessed.

Collecting a light wrap, she thought indignantly that being kissed by Alex had somehow turned her into a different person—a woman irritatingly sensitive to his every look, to every inflection in his deep voice. A woman who found herself sighing over the way the corners of his mouth turned up whenever he smiled—even the shape of his ears and the fact that the sun struck glints of red from his black hair!

Neither she nor Alex wanted a drink before dinner, so they went straight in to their meal. The woman who brought in the dishes was introduced as Caroline

Summers, the housekeeper. In her mid-thirties, she had a pleasant smile and a briskly competent manner that Serina liked.

And she was a brilliant cook. Suddenly hungry, Serina applied herself to an entrée of grilled mussels with bacon and almonds.

'It's one of my favourites,' Alex said, 'and I noticed you enjoyed seafood at the dinner for the wedding party, so I assumed you'd like this.'

After one mouthful she said enthusiastically, 'It's delicious. Is it a New Zealand favourite?'

'I don't know where Caroline found the recipe, or if she made it up. Ask her when she comes back. One of these days I'm probably going to lose her to a restaurant, but in the meantime she seems content enough to stay here while her children are young. Her husband is the livestock manager on the station.'

'The station?' she enquired.

'In New Zealand and Australia a large farm is called a station.'

Grateful for the neutral subject, Serina asked questions diligently while they ate, enjoying the sound of his voice, the sight of his lean, tanned hands across the table, the warmth from the flames in the fireplace, the silence of the darkening countryside...

She learned that Haruru had been his father's inheritance, that his mother had been the link through which Alex was related to Gerd and his brother Kelt—they shared the same New Zealand great-grandfather. And she deduced that, while Alex called the station home, the corporation he ran kept him too busy to spend much time there.

She learned that Haruru in Maori meant rumbling.

'There's a waterfall in the hills that can be heard rumbling through the ground for some distance,' Alex told her.

'How?'

'It's volcanic land, and it's probably a trick of acoustics.'

Above all, she learned that the delicious irritant of her attraction to him had deepened, turning into something darker and more dangerous—something that might teach her the meaning of heartbreak...

CHAPTER SIX

THAT night Serina slept well and the next morning Alex showed her around his garden, but for the first time ever she couldn't fully concentrate on the beauty and harmony of flowers and foliage and form. Her attention was fixed on the man beside her.

She wondered dismally if this—*whatever*—she felt for Alex was going to destroy her pleasure in gardens.

Not that it could be love. The mere thought of that shocked her.

She couldn't afford to love him. He'd made his attitude brutally clear; the unfulfilled desire that pulsated between them indicated a relationship, nothing more.

It was a relief to get into the Land Rover for a quick overview of the station. The track wound up to an airstrip along a ridge, providing a magnificent view over green hills and bush-clad gullies and the Pacific Ocean, a wide stretch of brilliant blue under the bright winter sky.

'Tomorrow we'll go down to the nearest beach,' he told her on their way back to the homestead. 'I hope you have some warm clothes with you?'

'Of course I have,' she returned crisply. 'But you don't need to entertain me, you know. Tomorrow I'll see about hiring a car so I can visit some of the gardens in the guidebook you found for me.'

He gave her a narrow glance. 'Have you ever driven on the left?'

'Oh, yes,' she said absently, trying not to look down the hill. Although the track was well-maintained, the ground fell away sharply on her side without any barrier and she refused to let him see how nervous she was. Heights intimidated her.

But he must have sensed it because he slowed the Land Rover down. 'When? And how much?'

Warmed by his unspoken consideration, she said, 'I used to visit Doran at his school in England. Also, when our nanny was ill I drove down to Somerset quite frequently to visit her.'

And on other occasions when she'd been checking out gardens and interviewing their owners.

He said, 'So you're experienced on both sides of the road.'

'And I'm a careful driver.' Scrupulously, she added, 'I did once set off from an intersection and head straight towards the wrong side. I was lucky—there was no other traffic, but it scared me and I've been super-cautious ever since.'

'If there had been other traffic you'd probably have kept to the left,' Alex said. He glanced at her. 'You don't need to hire a car; I'll drive you around.'

'I can't ask you to do that,' she protested, hiding her quick flare of pleasure.

'You didn't,' he said, reacting instantly when a bird sunning itself in the gravel flew up suddenly in front of the Land Rover.

Serina's sharp intake of breath wasn't necessary.

Without stamping on the brake, Alex slowed the vehicle but held it to the line.

'Never try to avoid a bird or an animal,' he said calmly. 'Probably more people have been killed taking abrupt evasive action than actually hitting something. Always stay on the road, and on your side if it's a public road.'

'Surely it's human instinct to try not to hurt anything?' she protested, feeling her tense muscles relax.

'Control it. You're good at control.'

Serina flushed. Except when he touched her...

He added, 'Unless you're faced with hitting another person and, even then, you need to weigh the consequences.'

Soberly, she said, 'I hope I never have to.' She returned to the original subject. 'But you don't need to drive me—you must have plenty of things to do without that. I'll buy a good map and I'm capable of finding my way around.'

'I can spare the time.'

When she began to object again, he said, 'Serina, I know lots more people—and gardens—than whoever wrote that guidebook, and most of them aren't open to the public.'

Serina was torn. She had to make this visit worthwhile, which meant seeing as many gardens as she could fit in. The more material she gathered, the better.

For *worthwhile* read profitable, she thought as the track they were on joined another wider and more travelled one.

But the real reason for her reluctance to have Alex for a chauffeur was the intensity of her response to him.

Thoughtfully, she said, 'There are occasions when you sound like my father in his most aristocratic mood.'

His tone matching hers, he responded, 'I do not feel in the least like your father.' After a taut few seconds he added dryly, 'Or your brother.'

She glanced sideways, her heart thumping erratically as she took in his autocratic profile. He might not work on the station, but his hands on the wheel were strong and competent. Some wicked part of her mind flashed up an image of them stroking slowly across her pale skin. Heat flamed deep within her, and she had to stare stonily ahead and concentrate on a flock of sheep in the field.

'One of them is cast,' Alex said, and brought the Land Rover to a stop.

Serina opened her door and scrambled down too, eyes on the sheep lying in the grass, its legs sticking out pathetically. 'What's the matter with it?' she asked as Alex swung lithely over the wire fence.

He set off towards the animal. 'It's heavy with wool and couldn't get up, and now its balance has gone. It will die if it's left like that. Stay there—I can deal with it.'

But Serina climbed the fence too, making sure she kept close to the post as he had done. The wires hurt her hands a little; she rubbed them down her jeans as she joined him. The rest of the flock scattered at their approach, but they stopped a safe distance away and turned to eye the two intruders curiously as Alex strode over to the struggling sheep.

It didn't seem likely that he'd need help but, just in case, Serina followed him across the short grass.

The sheep registered its dislike of being approached by bleating weakly and struggling. Serina watched as Alex bent and, without seeming to exert much effort, turned the animal so that it stood. It panted and hung its head, but seemed stable enough until he stepped back.

'Damn,' he muttered as it staggered. He grabbed it and held it steady.

Serina said, 'If we both hold it for a while until it gets its balance, would that help?'

'Probably, but you'd get dirty.' His voice held a sardonic note.

'So?' Irritated, she positioned herself beside the panting animal and pressed her knee against it. Greasy wool, warm from the winter sun, clung to the denim of her jeans.

'It smells,' he said, adding, 'and the wool will leave unfiltered, dirty lanolin on your hands and clothes. Those extremely well-cut jeans may never be the same again.'

'I've smelt a lot worse than this,' she said, meeting his eyes.

'In that case, thanks for helping,' he said coolly. 'They're due to be shorn today, so if we can get it steady it will be all right.'

It was oddly intimate, standing there with the animal panting between them. Serina concealed a wry smile, wondering how many of the women who'd stayed at that beautiful homestead had got this close to a sheep.

And what would his business rivals and allies think if they could see him now? Clad in a plaid shirt with sleeves rolled up to reveal strongly muscular arms, and a pair of trousers in some hard-wearing fabric that showed off narrow hips and strongly muscled thighs, he stood with booted feet braced, taller than her by some inches.

Accustomed to looking most men in the eyes, Serina felt overshadowed, yet oddly protected.

The silence was weighted too heavily with awareness, and she found herself saying, 'I somehow got the impression that most farmers in New Zealand travel with packs of eager dogs.'

'Usually only one or two,' he told her.

A note in his deep, amused voice sent a thrill of excitement through her. Serina nodded and looked away, trying to concentrate on the sunny day, the sounds of birds she'd never heard before, the earthy smell of the sheep—*anything* to take her mind off Alex's nearness.

Nothing worked.

He said, 'And I'm not a farmer. I'm a businessman. I don't have a dog because I'm away a lot and dogs—like spouses—need companionship to be happy.'

'Is that why you haven't married?'

The moment the words emerged she wished she could unsay them. Tensely, she waited for a well-deserved snub.

But he replied coolly, 'No. When—if—I marry I'll organise my life differently. Why are you still obstinately single?'

'I've got plenty of time,' she said lamely, and risked a glance upwards.

She met crystalline steel-blue eyes that heated instantly. 'Indeed you have,' he said lazily. And smiled, the sort of disturbing smile that should have sent her fleeing.

Instead, it further stimulated her rioting senses. This attraction was mutual, and she'd already decided to let things happen, so why wasn't she flirting with him, letting him know in a subtle way that she was—

Well, what *was* she?

Ready sounded over-eager and, anyway, she didn't know that she was ready.

With a pang, she realised she wanted something

more solid and lasting than flirtation. She wanted to be wooed.

Like some Victorian maiden with a head stuffed full of unrealistic dreams, she scoffed. It didn't happen in her world, where people responded to strong attraction by embarking on an affair. Sometimes they married, but once the glamour became tarnished they called everything off, often to repeat the whole process with someone else.

Love was a temporary aberration, and marriage an alliance made for other, infinitely more practical reasons.

Except for rare, fortunate exceptions like Rosie and Gerd, of course. And, although she wished them every good thing in their life together, she couldn't help wondering how long Rosie's incandescent joy would last.

She looked up. Alex was watching her, and something about his waiting silence made her heart flip madly so that when she spoke her voice was husky and soft.

'What is it? Do I have lanolin on my face?'

Colour tinged her skin when he inspected her even more closely, but she held her gaze steady when he drawled, 'Not a speck on that exquisite skin. I was just admiring the way the sun strikes blue sparks off your hair. But I'll give you a hat when we get home—the sun can burn even in winter here.'

She swallowed. 'Thank you.'

'And it would be a crime to singe that exquisite skin.' Taking her by surprise, he bent his head and kissed the tip of her nose.

Eyes enormous in her face, Serina held her breath and froze. The sun suddenly seemed brighter, the colours more vivid, the unseen birds more piercingly musical. A wave of heat broke over her.

Until he straightened and said, 'We'll see if this old girl can stand up by herself now. Let her go and step slowly away.'

Fighting a fierce, foolish disappointment, Serina obeyed. The ewe lurched, but as Alex moved back she stood more firmly. After a few seconds she dropped her head and, ignoring them, began to crop the grass eagerly.

'She should be all right,' Alex said.

Serina didn't dare speak until they were well away, then she said, 'What will happen if she falls again?'

'I'll tell Caroline's husband and he'll make sure someone keeps an eye on this mob.'

He reached out and took her hand. Serina almost stumbled, heart pounding as they finished the walk back to the Land Rover.

The fence negotiated, Alex leant past her to open the door but, before she could get in, he slid an arm around her and held her loosely, his eyes intent.

Serina's breath locked in her throat. Mutely, wondering how on earth other women signalled that they'd decided they were ready for an affair, she followed the instinct that prompted a sigh, then turned her head into the strong tanned column of his throat, unconsciously letting her lips linger on his skin.

Alex's big frame hardened, sending fierce little shivers through her, but he made no attempt to tighten his embrace. In a voice that alerted every nerve, he said, 'Sure, Serina?'

'Absolutely.' The word sounded faint and faraway, so to make sure there could be no doubt she lifted her head, her lips curving in a smile that hinted at a sultry promise when her smoky gaze met the narrowed, glittering intensity of Alex's. 'Are you always going to ask me if I'm sure?'

'Until I'm sure of *you*.'

Her stomach dropped several inches, but it was too late for any second thoughts. He bent his head and kissed her.

The kiss was everything she'd been secretly craving, a passionate seal on their almost wordless pact. Her tumbling thoughts vanished under the barely leashed sensuality of his mouth as he showed her just what his kiss could do.

The arm across her back slid downwards, catching her hips and pulling them against him. His fierce response to the erotic pressure made her gasp, and he immediately took advantage, claiming more than her lips, his deep, deep kisses carrying her into some unknown world of the senses where all she could feel was the rising urgency of her own needs and a fierce, unbelievable hunger.

Abandoning herself to desire, she pressed against him, some unknown part of her relishing the unchained compulsion to lose herself entirely in this dazzling, sensuous world.

It came as a shock when he lifted his head and said in a voice that rasped with a blend of passion and frustration, 'Someone's coming.'

Sure enough, when he let her go Serina registered the sound of an engine. Another vehicle was heading towards them along the track.

Alex held her for a moment as she struggled for balance—just like the ewe, she thought half-hysterically. He frowned as he looked above her head and let his hands drop. 'Lindy.'

Taking what tiny comfort she could from the narrow

frown between his brows, Serina realised she wasn't surprised. With the intuition of a woman in an equivocal situation, she'd realised that Lindy wanted Alex. They might have been brought up as brother and sister, but that wasn't how Lindy saw him.

Serina tried to feel sorry for her, but she couldn't prevent a cold prickle of foreboding when she met the other woman's flat stare as she drew up beside them in a sleek, only slightly dusty ute.

'What on earth are you two up to?' Lindy asked through the window.

Alex nodded towards the sheep, all watching them. 'One of them was cast,' he said. 'We got her on her feet, but she's still shaky.'

'Oh, poor Serina,' Lindy said with a glittery smile. 'What an introduction to the place! Smelly old sheep aren't in the least romantic, are they? Never mind—get Alex to take you out to dinner.'

She waved an airy hand and shot off, scattering stones.

Alex said, 'Would you like to go out to dinner?'

Not at Lindy's behest she wouldn't!

'I don't think that would be a good idea,' Serina hedged. 'Although I slept like a top last night, I'm feeling a bit washed out right now.'

The glint in his eyes told her he was amused, but he said soberly, 'Then we'll have a quiet meal at home tonight and see how you feel tomorrow.'

But the other woman's arrival had somehow cast a cloud over the afternoon.

Back at the homestead, Serina thanked him, then said, 'I'd like to try my camera out in your garden, if that's all right with you?'

'I don't want you writing about my garden,' he said crisply.

'I know, and I won't, but I'll want to take photographs when I visit other gardens, and the light here, especially during the middle of the day, is very clear and stark. I'd like to work out what settings are best.'

He held her eyes a second longer than necessary, then nodded. 'Have you always taken your own photographs?'

'Not at the beginning, but I do now,' she said a little aloofly, still chilled by his initial distrust. 'When I was working for Rassel I became interested in photography, so I soaked up as much knowledge about the way professional photographers do it as I could. I was lucky— one in particular used to critique my shots.' She gave a slight smile. 'He was cruel, but I learned an awful lot from him.'

His mouth thinned, then relaxed. 'I have a few calls to answer,' he said, 'so I'll be busy for an hour or so. Enjoy the garden.'

Still on edge, Serina collected her camera and went out into the garden again. The flowers in a wide border glowed as she relived Alex's kisses and their explosive effect on her.

He'd kissed her like a lover, she thought dreamily.

She walked beneath a huge tree and closed her eyes for a moment.

Of course she wasn't his lover. If it existed, true love had to mean you knew the person you loved, trusted them deeply and intimately and were completely convinced they'd never let you down.

Like Rosie and Gerd. They'd known each other since they were children. Whereas she'd only met Alex a few

times before she'd embarked on this crazy trip across
the world with him.

Yes, she'd felt an instant attraction, and been strangely
elated to realise he felt it too. And she'd trusted him
enough to come to New Zealand with him, she reminded
herself and bit her lip—then muttered, 'Ouch!' when her
teeth grazed the tender skin there.

When Alex kissed a woman she certainly knew she'd
been kissed, she thought, trying to find some humour to
lighten her mood.

But his reaction when she'd suggested she take photographs of his garden showed her how little he trusted
her. Tension wound her tight, set her pacing restlessly
out into the sunlight, still warm but now thickening into
a gold that edged close to amber as the sun sank towards
the hills to the west.

It was stupid to feel hurt. Alex certainly wasn't in love
with her, so why did she expect him to trust her?

Because what she felt for him—all she could allow
herself to feel—was a mad, wild, unreasonable desire.
Just *thinking* of him made her body spring into instant
life, as though charged with electricity, and when she was
with him she teetered on the most deliciously terrifying
tenterhooks, so aware of his every movement that it was
almost a relief to walk away.

Lust, she told herself sternly. Not love…

'Forget about him,' she told herself, startling a small
bird with a tail like a fan into darting upwards. It landed
on a tall stem a few feet away and surveyed her with
black button eyes, scolding her with high-pitched chirps
as it flirted its tail at her.

Smiling, she lifted her camera and got a shot of it,

using it to get some pointers on how to deal with the bright, clear light.

But, try as she did to concentrate on photographic techniques, her obstinate mind kept replaying the way Alex had held her hand as they'd walked back to the Land Rover.

Somehow, that most casual of caresses meant more—just *more*, she thought in confusion.

Not more than his kisses, which had rocked her world, yet in a strange way that casual linking of hands satisfied something she didn't recognise in herself, a kind of yearning...

For what?

She shook her head. Romance?

Giving up, she went inside and inspected her shots, relieved when several showed up really well—so well, she emailed a couple to her editor as a sample of what was in store for her.

Then she surveyed her clothes, finally choosing a little black dress. Discretion itself, she thought satirically. Ladylike and quite forgettable, although it did nice things for her skin and eyes.

And it was useless to wish now she'd brought something more daring, something that would subtly signal the change in her. Pulling a face at her reflection, she combed back her hair and caught it behind her head with a neat, unobtrusive clip. It didn't seem likely that for a quiet dinner for two at home Alex would dress too formally, but she had no idea what New Zealanders wore for such occasions.

Or even if it mattered. Last night she'd changed into a pair of tailored silk trousers and a simple soft blouse, relieved when Alex had been equally casually attired.

And it was foolish to think anything had altered just because he'd kissed her again, and she'd somehow— she hoped—managed to convey how much she wanted him.

Butterflies swirled through her stomach when she left her room, setting up a frenzied internal tornado when Alex came through a door a few metres along the wide hallway. To her relief, he was clad informally in a well-tailored linen shirt and narrow-cut trousers that set off the powerful body beneath.

Without trying to hide the gleam of appreciation in his eyes, he said, 'Tell me, is it training or do you somehow just know the perfect way to look for any occasion?'

Colour heated her skin, but she managed to say demurely, 'What a lovely compliment.'

He laughed and opened a door into a room that looked more like a library than a study. Standing back to let her go in first, he said, 'That is no answer.'

'Because your question was unanswerable. I choose what I hope will be appropriate for the occasion and leave it at that.'

He surveyed her through his lashes. 'And an elegant, very chic *that* it is tonight.'

His response washed a deeper tinge of colour through her translucent skin. For a moment the violet eyes were clouded by an emotion Alex couldn't define.

They cleared almost instantly and she said, 'I wonder why I have the feeling you're testing me in some subtle way I don't understand?'

He already knew she wasn't the stock princess he'd first thought, but he was surprised she'd dropped her usual reserve for such a forthright statement. Ignoring a sharp rush of adrenalin, he said, 'You have an overactive imagination. I like to see you blush—it's a charming reaction.'

How many other men had summoned that swift, rapidly fading heat? The photographer who'd been cruel but helpful? That thought brought with it a fierce, baseless anger that startled him.

He asked, 'What would you like to drink?'

After a cool glance she said, 'Wine would be great, thank you.'

To her surprise, he opened a bottle of champagne-style wine. Pouring it for her, he said, 'This is from the Hawkes Bay, a big wine-growing region. Like Aura and Flint, most Northland vineyards tend to concentrate on growing for red wines. Some vintners buy in grapes to make their white wines. In the far north there are several vineyards, some of them with magnificent grounds. I've included them in a list of places you might find interesting. You can look at it after dinner, and tomorrow I'll contact any you'd like to see.'

She took a sip of the liquid. Alex watched the curve of her artfully coloured mouth as it kissed the glass, and felt his gut tighten. Cynically he thought that for someone who'd never put a foot wrong, never figured in any scandal, she certainly knew all the tricks.

And she kissed like a houri. She'd learned that from someone. Or several someones. So his Princess was nothing if not discreet.

For no reason—because she *wasn't* his Princess—the thought burned like acid.

Serina set her champagne flute down and met his eyes, her gaze level. 'You're being very helpful,' she said, 'but I'd feel better if I contacted them.'

'People here know who I am,' he said matter-of-factly. 'Like it or not, it does make a difference.'

A steely note in her voice, she answered, 'I realise that, and of course I'm grateful for the offer, but I'm not accustomed to being sponsored.'

Alex had researched her work, concentrating on places he'd visited himself, and been surprised to discover she had a rare skill for evoking the soul of a garden. For a reason he wasn't going to inspect too deeply, her refusal to accept his help sparked his temper.

'With respect,' he said sardonically, 'I suggest you stop cutting off your nose to spite your face. This is New Zealand, and although I'm sure the magazine you write for has some readers here, it's probably not enough to make you famous.'

'I didn't—'

He overrode her protest. 'It will be much easier for you if I do stand sponsor to you—and at least the owners will know you won't be casing their properties for a future robbery.'

Her head came up proudly. 'As if that's likely to happen,' she retorted scornfully, her eyes sparkling with outrage.

Alex shrugged. 'New Zealand has a low level of crime, but we're not free of it. You can't blame people if they are a little suspicious of an unknown person who not only asks if she can come and check out their properties, but brings a camera with her.'

She frowned, and before she could speak he went on levelly, 'In your world, Princess, you're very well known. Here, you're not. I am.'

He waited while she absorbed that, watching her frown smooth out and her thoughtful nod.

Slowly, she said, 'Of course. I didn't mean to be presumptuous.' She looked at him. 'I've just realised I have a confession to make—I took photographs of your garden and sent them to my editor as an indication of what gardens are like here. I'm sorry, I'll get her to delete them.'

Irritated, he said shortly, 'Just make sure she doesn't publish them.'

'She knows they're not for publication.'

She took another sip of her wine and this time he watched deliberately, noting the way she tasted—as though she was an expert.

Perfectly trained, he thought, and wondered why, when he wanted so urgently to kiss the wine from her lips, to feel the soft meltdown of her body against his, all he could do was search for flaws. Just looking at her was enough to scramble his brain, and he couldn't afford to allow this unusual desire to overwhelm his common sense.

Only an hour ago he'd spoken to Gerd on the secure line and discovered that, although Doran seemed more than happy to explore the delights of Vanuatu wrecks and reefs, his band of gaming companions had turned up in one of the coastal towns in the border region of Carathia and Montevel.

Ostensibly on holiday.

Had Princess Serina made the somewhat surprising decision to come to New Zealand in order to throw any suspicious person off the scent? He had every reason to believe her brother had gone to Vanuatu for just that reason. That afternoon Gerd had told Alex that the security man he'd sent to infiltrate the group had been overeager and raised suspicion. Alex had ordered the plant's immediate withdrawal, but from now on they'd have to work on the assumption that the group knew they'd been infiltrated.

How deeply in their confidence was Serina? She'd used her email that afternoon to send photographs. Had she contacted Doran, or the plotters?

He glanced down at her face, as serene as her name, beautiful and remote and desirably tempting.

Her explanation of her brother's activities had been almost believable, but she hadn't been persuasive enough to quite convince him. According to his man, there was an excellent chance she was fully aware of what was going on.

With the spy gone, he and Gerd had no other way of finding out anything more but, from what they'd learned, the plotters were getting ready to make a move.

Perhaps it was time to find out whether Serina was ready to sacrifice her body to the cause.

He forced back an instinctive distaste. Lives would be lost if the group were allowed to proceed and, although he had no sympathy for those who believed the end justified the means, he suspected this was one of the times when it really did.

Besides, although Serina was extremely aware of him, she was no fluttering ingénue, hoping that an affair would lead to marriage. Her father, a notorious libertine, would have taught her that such things were transitory.

And he wouldn't be faking. From the moment he'd met her, he'd found the aloof Princess Serina very alluring and he was enjoying crossing swords with her.

Plenty of very satisfactory relationships, he thought cynically, had been built on much more shaky grounds than that.

CHAPTER SEVEN

MADE wary and somewhat confused by Alex's silence, Serina took another sip of wine.

He said calmly, 'So it's agreed then that I'll make the first contact, and I'll come with you.'

Why was she hesitating? His suggestion made sense, yet some recalcitrant part of her urged her to be cautious, to cling to her independence. And long periods spent with Alex in the close confines of a car would dangerously weaken her resistance.

What resistance?

In his arms she'd completely surrendered, offering him anything he wanted. What would have happened if Lindy hadn't come along?

Nothing, she thought sturdily. Alex was super-sophisticated; she couldn't imagine him making love in a Land Rover, or on the grass in full view of a mob of sheep…

The thought should have made her smile. Instead, heat curled up through her, seductive and taunting. Imposing rigid constraint on her treacherous thoughts, she said, 'Yes. Thank you very much for being so helpful.'

Something moved in the depths of his eyes and his smile held a touch of mockery, as though he understood her reluctance and found it amusing. However, his tone was almost formal. 'It will be my pleasure. How are you enjoying that wine?'

'It's delicious.'

'Someone taught you how to evaluate it.'

She set the glass down. 'My father was a true connoisseur and did his best to make sure Doran and I were too.'

Her father's cellar and her mother's jewels had helped pay off his debts after her parents had been killed. Selling the villa, with its magnificent gardens, hadn't been enough. The only things she'd been able to salvage were her mother's tiara—paste, she'd discovered to her shock—and her father's telescope.

'So I've heard,' Alex said.

A note in his voice made Serina wonder what else he'd heard about her father. That he was also a great connoisseur of women?

Ignoring the cynical thought, she said lightly, 'And of course anyone who likes wine knows that New Zealand produces really interesting, fresh vintages that have won some top competitions.'

She relaxed when they moved on to more general topics. Alex's keen mind fascinated her, and she quickly learned to respect his breadth of knowledge.

Yet his every word, each disturbing look from those ice-blue eyes, was enriched by an undercurrent of muted, potent sensuality. Focused on her, hot and intense, it sharpened her senses into an unbearably exciting awareness of everything about him—from the deep timbre of his voice to the lithe masculine grace of his movements.

During the superb meal and coffee in the library afterwards, Serina was not only aware of a smouldering arousal, but was shocked to find herself unconsciously sending subtly flirtatious glances his way.

Enough, she commanded after a pause that had gone on too long. Much more of this, and you'll be asking him to kiss you again.

Or take you to bed...

But it took a huge effort of will to uncoil herself from an elderly and extremely comfortable leather sofa in front of the fireplace and say huskily, 'I suspect I haven't entirely got over jet lag. I know I should try to stay awake, but I'm going to drop off to sleep right here if I don't go.'

He got to his feet. The renewed impact of his height and the fluid power of his body stirred a heady stimulation more potent than the champagne she'd drunk before dinner.

Terrified that he'd recognise her chaotic mixture of need and longing, she kept her gaze fixed on the arrogant jut of his jaw and dredged up enough composure to say almost steadily, 'Thank you for a delicious meal and a very pleasant evening.'

But, when she turned to go, a hand on her shoulder froze her into stillness. Heart juddering into overdrive, she opened her mouth to object, then closed it again and allowed herself to be eased around to face him.

Their eyes duelled—his narrowed in an intent, direct challenge so forceful she shivered.

'Tell me what you want,' he said, each word harsh and distinct.

She swallowed and nodded, stunned at her trust in this man she barely knew. 'You already know,' she said in a tone she'd never used before.

His chest rose and fell. Mindlessly, she swayed into his arms as they closed around her.

'Look at me,' he commanded, his voice low and raw.

Serina obeyed, and abandoned the final remnants of caution when she saw his gaze heat with a blaze of desire.

It was far too soon to surrender, she thought vaguely, but when his mouth claimed hers her mind closed down, yielding to the pure carnal rapture of sensation, releasing the barriers of her will to let her body enjoy what it craved—had craved so desperately since their first kiss.

No, even before that, although she'd rarely let herself admit it. Their first meeting a year ago had sparked a hunger that the long months apart had only increased.

His lips opened on hers, coaxing and persuasive. Shivering deliciously at the silent invitation, she accepted it. His tongue plunged, and she wriggled against him, her body insistently demanding a satisfaction she'd never yet experienced.

Alex's arms tightened, bringing her into intimate, explosive contact with the hardness of his loins. Rivulets of fire ran through her, turning into ashes all the convictions that had kept her a virgin.

He lifted his head. Serina sighed, turned her face into his neck and sank her teeth lightly into his skin.

'Serina.'

The way he said her name—in a voice raw with passion—sounded more wonderful to her than the most exquisite music. She kissed the tanned, subtly flavoured skin she'd bitten, inhaling the faint sensuous scent that was his alone. A shudder flexed his lean body and she felt the latent power there, the male strength she both desired and feared.

'Alex,' she said softly and, in her own language, the language of her ancestors, she murmured, 'Your kiss has stolen my soul...'

'What are you saying?'

Realisation iced through her. How could she have been so swept away as to come out with that? Shocked, she overcame her reckless need sufficiently to say tonelessly, 'It's something from an old Montevellan folk song. My first nurse used to sing it to me...'

The words faltered in her mouth and she could have bitten her tongue out. If this was what lust did to you—unlocked the bars of your mind so that all the secrets came spilling out—it was terrifying.

And love had to be even worse—a total revelation. How could anyone bear it? Closing her eyes, she turned her head away.

'Translate it for me,' Alex said.

Ever since she'd been old enough to realise the depths of passion in the simple words, she'd refused to believe anyone could feel so desperately lost to desire. Now she'd known that same reckless capitulation, she understood, and the knowledge locked her lips.

A lean finger turned her head, tilted it. She forced her eyelids up, braced herself to meet and repel the leashed authority of his gaze.

'Serina?'

And, when she couldn't move, he said, 'All right, you don't want to tell me, but you can come out of hiding.'

Shrugging, she tried for a smile. It wobbled precariously, but she managed to say in a reasonably level voice, 'It's nothing, really. Take the music away and it turns into the usual treacly sentiments you find in every pop song. And I'm not going to sing it to you!'

She felt his chest lift, and his quiet laughter reverberated against her. 'It seems only poets can do true justice to our deepest emotions. Whatever was said in your old song, it's entirely mutual.'

Swift and sure, he kissed her. His previous kisses had taken her to an unknown place where the rules she'd lived her life by were shattered. This one was so frankly carnal it set her head reeling. Her mouth softened under his, opened again.

A prisoner of dangerous need, she melted into him, taking reckless delight in the harsh intake of his breath. Whatever he felt, she thought with her last remnant of logic, he couldn't hide his hunger.

When he lifted his head she tensed, thinking he was going to stop, but he transferred his attention to her throat, and after he'd found the vulnerable hollow at the base he trailed kisses across the silken skin to reach the acutely sensitive spot at the junction of her neck and shoulder.

Her knees buckled at the sensation—urgent and savagely consuming—that drowned her in molten pleasure, singing through her body with a primal magnetic summons.

His teeth grazed her skin, repeating the erotic little caress she'd given him. Sensation stormed through her. In her innermost heart Serina realised that she had been born for his touch.

Born for this man...

Panic clogged her throat.

Alex raised his head. Half-closed gaze holding her

still, he shifted one hand to cup a pleading, sensitised breast.

Anticipation, wild and feverishly sweet, clamoured through Serina. Unable to bear the intensity of it, stunned by the discovery she'd just made, she let her lashes droop to hide her eyes.

But he commanded, 'Look at me.'

Barely able to articulate, she whispered, 'It's too much…'

'It's not enough,' he rasped.

'Alex,' she muttered, unable to say anything more, clinging to his name as a life-raft in this turbulent sea of emotional discovery.

He lowered his head again and took her mouth.

The kiss was urgent and compelling. Inside, she became hot and slick, her body preparing her for the ultimate embrace. For a fleeting moment she stiffened but, when his other hand found her hips and eased her even closer, she knew that if she didn't follow where her heart led she'd always regret it. No matter what happened, what lay ahead, she wanted this—wanted *Alex*—with a desperation that made rejection unthinkable.

Her breath stopped in her lungs as his thumb moved slowly, lightly across the nub of her breast, sending jagged white-hot darts of excitement through her.

She needed…something else; without volition, her back arched, pressing the curve of her breast into his palm.

His smile taut and humourless, Alex repeated the small movement. Its impact went right down to her toes, sizzling from nerve to nerve and melting her spine. A soft, erotic little sound in her throat startled her.

He had to be able to hear—and feel—the thunder of

her heart as her breasts lifted and fell more and more rapidly, in time with the tormenting glide of his thumb over the acutely sensitive centre.

Waves of pleasure swelled through her in intolerable yearning. Buttressing them was an emotion even stronger and more durable than this shimmering, incandescent desire.

Somehow, without realising it, she'd fallen in love with Alex.

Knowing full well that it wasn't returned...

Dimly, Serina knew she should be afraid, shocked, bewildered—should feel *anything* other than this sensuous delight that gave her the courage to raise her lashes when the kiss had finished.

Alex's eyes gleamed like midnight sapphires in the bronzed, autocratic angles of his face. Her pulse rocketed when she saw the evidence of her fierce response to his kisses on his mouth—both the thinner top lip and the sensuous curve of the bottom were fuller than normal.

Her hands had somehow worked themselves across his back. She let them quest further down, her body tightening in exquisite supplication when she felt his response beneath her palms. Emboldened, she went further, only to freeze when the powerful thigh muscles stirred against her.

His eyes blazed a question.

Colour burned across her skin. With a lingering kiss to his throat, she signalled her wordless agreement but he demanded, 'You're sure?'

'Very sure.' Could that be her voice, vibrant with languorous promise?

But should she tell him that this was very new to her?

It seemed only fair, although a cloud darkened the surface of her excitement. After nervously wetting her lips, she muttered, 'I haven't…haven't actually…'

'You're not protected?' He held her away from him, his expression difficult to read. 'Don't worry about that,' he said swiftly and hugged her. 'I can deal with it.'

Her eager anticipation dimmed a little more. Of course he would have protection. No doubt his other lovers had spent time with him in this house—although they, she thought on a pang of sharp jealousy, had probably slept in the big bed she'd glimpsed in his room.

Alex said, 'But not here, I think. Would you like time to get ready?'

No, she would not; it might give her time to rethink this. And if she did that she'd always regret it.

She looked at him with something like challenge. 'Like a Victorian bride?' she said, then wondered what trick from her unconscious had brought that to mind.

Because *bridal* was exactly how she felt—a little afraid, more than a little self-conscious, and yet eager, longing for what was going to happen.

And she still hadn't let him know that she was totally inexperienced.

She opened her mouth again to do so, but he stopped the tumbling words with a kiss, and under that passionate onslaught she forgot what she'd been going to say, forgot everything but the elemental need to make love to him.

When he lifted his head she leaned into him to kiss his throat again. Daringly, she licked the place she'd just kissed, savouring the essence of him.

'Hardly a Victorian bride,' he said unevenly. 'Your bedroom, I think.'

Her acquiescence turned into a squeak when he swung her up into his arms.

'I'm too heavy,' she protested.

'You're tall, but far from heavy.'

His smile revealed a flash of sheer male pleasure in his strength and, held against his heart, Serina felt more secure than she'd ever been in her life.

Outside her room, he slid her down his body and held her for a moment before turning the door handle. Inside, the room was warmed by the glow from the lamp on the bedside table.

Serina went in ahead and turned, holding the door wide. 'Welcome,' she said in a smoky little voice, and immediately felt foolish.

This was his house, after all.

But he said, 'Thank you,' as though he understood the obscure impulse that had summoned the words. And then he said with a wry twist of his lips, 'I'll leave you here for a few seconds.'

Of course. Protection...

Why hadn't he chosen his bedroom to make love to her? Serina closed the door behind him and stared sightlessly around the beautifully furnished room. Perhaps he liked his privacy, she thought with a hint of hysteria.

She had no idea how to behave, probably for the first time since childhood—and now there was no mother, no governess to school her.

This was just her and the man she loved, the man she wanted with all her heart and with every importunate cell in her body.

A tap on the door made her start. She swung around and after a cowardly second opened it.

Awkwardness overwhelmed her. Fixing her eyes on

the middle of Alex's chest, she searched desperately for something to say, finally coming out with, 'When I was a child my nurse always left the light on so I never went into a dark room.'

'Because of the nightmares?'

She nodded. 'I'm afraid I still make sure of it, even though I know I shouldn't waste power.'

'Your peace of mind is as important as saving electricity,' he said quietly. 'Why are you looking so intently at my button?'

The question jerked her head up, as perhaps he'd hoped it would, and her knees buckled under the heat of his gaze.

'It's a very nice button,' she said idiotically.

He took her hand and placed it squarely over the button so that the heavy, fast thud of his heartbeat reverberated into her palm.

'Perhaps you'd like to undo it,' he suggested, a hint of laughter in his tone surprising her, and somehow relieving a little of her shyness.

She accepted the challenge, then with great daring slid her hand into the opening she'd made. Excitement flared within her at the immediate increase in his pulse rate.

'See what you do to me?' he asked roughly.

His skin was hot and taut, a fine scroll of hair giving it texture above a firm contrasting layer of muscle. Serina luxuriated in the novelty of exploring him, and bravely undid the button above the first. When he made no objection, she freed the one above that too.

'You might as well finish the job,' he said when she hesitated.

Head bent, she did just that, then pushed the shirt back

from his shoulders and drew in a long uneven breath at what her fingers revealed.

The only word her dazed mind could come up with was *magnificent*. The lamplight gleamed richly on supple, sleek skin, lovingly burnishing the clean, strong lines of him. Next to him, she felt small, delicate, even fragile. She couldn't speak, couldn't think and her hands shook as they fell to her sides.

Almost immediately, he reached for her and said into her hair, 'My sweet girl, don't be afraid.'

'I'm not,' she blurted. 'I'm—I'm overwhelmed.'

She kissed his shoulder, then remembered the caress he'd given her—only a few minutes ago, yet she felt she'd come so far since then—and raised her hand to flick her thumb across one tight male nipple.

His sharply indrawn breath filled her with delight. He tilted her face so that he could see her, and she met his narrowed blazing eyes with something like a challenge in her own.

'I'm glad,' he said smoothly. 'And now it's my turn to be overwhelmed.'

He unzipped the back of her dress and unhooked her bra with an ease that showed how familiar he was with a woman's clothes—with a woman's body. Ignoring the pang that thought gave her, she took refuge in silence when the dress fell free of her shoulders, revealing the black silk bra and briefs that hugged a narrow waist and slender hips.

'You are...utterly, dangerously beautiful,' he said, each word raw, as though torn from him.

Colour burned up from her breasts and heated her cheekbones.

Scanning legs clad in sheer black and the high-heeled

courts she'd packed because of their versatility, he said, 'You might be more comfortable if you take off the shoes.'

It was easy enough to kick them off, but she gasped when he dropped to his knees and eased the stockings from her legs. His hands stroked up again from her calf to her thighs, lingering a few seconds on the satin skin there. Pierced by uncontrollable bliss, Serina shivered.

Alex looked up, his hard-hewn face tense. The smile that curved his mouth was just short of savage, and she shivered again.

He got to his feet with less than his usual litheness, towering over her for a charged moment until he turned away abruptly.

Hot anticipation pooled in the pit of Serina's stomach. Still unable to speak, she watched the muscles in his wide shoulders coil as he hauled back the covers of the bed. Uncertain, yet aware that she'd arrived at a place she'd never known she wanted to be, she stood tall, meeting his eyes with something close to anxiety when he straightened up.

It seemed he understood her shyness because he drew her into his arms, shielding her from his gaze with his own body. He bent his head, but this time his lips found the soft swell of her breast.

Ardent anticipation drummed through her. Enthralled, she dragged in a gasping impeded breath. He flicked the bra free and when she automatically tried to cover herself with her forearms he said, 'That's a crime, Serina.'

She gaped at him, and he smiled. 'A crime,' he repeated, his voice rough, and added as he reached for her, 'like covering the Venus de Milo with sackcloth...'

He forestalled her instinctive step backwards by

picking her up and carrying her across to deposit her carefully on the bed. Serina had to stop herself from huddling the sheet over her almost nude body when he looked down at her, heat kindling in the dark depths of his eyes.

Yet, in spite of her embarrassment, the roving survey of his gaze warmed her, stirred her excitement to fever-pitch. Desire clamoured up through her, but she managed a smile that held more than a hint of challenge. 'I'm beginning to suspect you're shy.'

Laughing, and without obvious haste or embarrassment, Alex shucked off the rest of his clothes.

Serina fought back the shock that almost saw her close her eyes. She wanted—*needed*—to see him without sophisticated tailoring and superb fabrics.

Naked, he was a warrior, she thought hazily. Big body poised and intent, something in his eyes, in his stark, stripped features, in the primal power of his body made her think of a more primitive age.

In a thin voice, she broke the charged silence. 'I feel like plunder.'

He said abruptly, 'I'm no pirate, Serina.'

'I know that.' She held out her hands, fingers slipping lightly over his heated skin, a smile trembling on her lips. 'You don't have to keep reassuring me.'

Serina had thought she knew quite a lot about making love; after all, she'd read about it, seen it acted out in movies and on television.

But nothing had—nothing could *ever* have—prepared her for Alex's caresses, his absorbed expression when he bent his head to her breasts, or the searing, surging flames that ignited every cell in her body as his mouth closed around the rosy aureole.

A groan was torn from her. Obeying an impulse as old as time, her body arched instinctively into him, taut as a bow, while he wrapped his arms around her. Closing her eyes against the unbearable enchantment of his love-making, she surrendered completely.

He took her on a wildfire journey of the senses— touch, taste, the faint erotic scent from their entwined bodies, the sight of his tanned hand against her white skin, the sound of his breathing when she mimicked his caresses and discovered the flexible line of his spine, the lean, potent strength so miraculously curbed in deference to her.

Sensation built and built inside, slowly at first, then with such ferocity that her breathing began to match his. Every muscle, every sinew tense with expectation, she craved an unknown satisfaction. When he found the little hollow of her navel with his tongue, she gave a gasping cry. Her body clenched, pushed upwards into him.

'Ah, you like that,' he said, and slid a hand down past her hips to cup the mound that ached for him.

Once again, her reaction was mindless—she jerked, thrusting herself against his delicately probing fingers, mutely demanding something…anything…

'Is this what you want?' he asked, guiding a lean finger inside her, his thumb performing magic on her.

Serina gasped, gripped by a roiling ecstasy, and her body took over, such rapture engulfing her that she had no idea she was almost sobbing as waves of unbearable pleasure forced her into fulfilment and then receded, leaving her replete and utterly relaxed.

Alex's arms around her were all she needed to feel utterly safe. He held her while she came down, and only then swung off the bed. Stunned, Serina opened her eyes to a slit, closing them again when she realised he was getting something from his trouser pocket.

She shivered. If he gave her nothing more than that, she thought, she'd still be grateful. But she was greedy now—she wanted more, to fully experience his possession, to take him into her and give him all she had, all she was.

The mattress sank slightly under his weight beside her and she turned into his arms with a confidence that banished all fear. One hand curved around the hard line of his jaw as he began to kiss her—gently at first, then with more passion when she responded with languorous ardour.

That new confidence persuaded her to make her own discoveries, trailing her hand down his chest and across the flat plane of his stomach.

But when she got too close he said thickly, 'Not now, Serina—not unless you're content with what you've already had. I'm not superhuman.'

She snatched her hand away, but he caught it and held it against his chest. 'Next time you can do what you like with me, but right now it would mean the end.'

'We wouldn't want that.' Her voice, throaty and seductive, startled her.

Alex moved over her. 'No,' he growled. Holding her gaze with his own, he lowered himself and in one steady thrust pushed into her.

Serina's body stiffened at the intrusion. His brows contracted and she realised he was going to pull away.

'*No,*' she said, clutching his shoulders. Consciously, desperately, she relaxed internal muscles she hadn't known existed.

To her incandescent joy, sensation returned in a rush,

filling her with fire. This time he eased into her, and when he met no resistance he drove deeper, and then even more deeply, each movement of his body a claim she couldn't resist, a bold statement that forced her further and further up a slope towards ecstasy.

When it came she sobbed again, only this time the rapture was so vehement, so overwhelming she was completely lost in it.

Only then did Alex give way to his own desire; awed and delighted all over again, she watched as he flung his head back. That control she thought so inborn a quality was etched into his face until he too surrendered and she saw it vanish under the same unbearable pleasure that still racked her.

And then it was over, and he went to ease himself off her.

'No,' she said, barely able to get the word out but determined not to let him go.

'I'm too big.'

'No,' she repeated, her arms constricting around him.

He looked down at her, the fierce flames dying in his eyes, and then yielded, letting her bear his comforting weight.

Happier than she had ever been in her life, yet acutely aware that her happiness was fragile and fleeting, Serina luxuriated in his care until she felt herself slipping into sleep.

She barely recognised the moment when he lifted himself from her; a murmured protest died away when he turned on his side and gathered her into his arms.

'Sleep now,' he said.

Her head on one strong shoulder, Serina allowed

herself one last glance at his face, one last sensation of sated delight before she turned her face into his shoulder and allowed exhaustion to overtake her.

CHAPTER EIGHT

SERINA woke and stretched, startled by the pleasant pull of muscles never previously used. She wasn't surprised to discover she was alone; somehow she must have registered Alex's departure in her sleep. A glance around the room told her it was light outside, and she could hear birds singing lustily in the gardens outside.

The dawn chorus, she thought dreamily, remembering his words.

In a way she was glad Alex had left. She needed time and solitude to sort out her emotions.

But, although she tried hard to concentrate, her thoughts kept drifting into memories, and after a while she gave up and just let herself float in their sensuous warmth. She'd had no idea that making love could be so...so *ultimate*.

Alex had been by turns tender and fierce, always passionate. She'd wondered what he would be like if he ever slipped the bonds of that control...

Now she knew.

Yet even at that climactic moment she hadn't felt wary or constrained, and he certainly hadn't treated her as an object, a mere vehicle to sate his desire.

As for a wildness to match her own complete surrender—well, Alex's self-possession was an integral part of him. It was as inborn as the polar blue of his eyes, the angles of that tough jaw, the timbre of his deep voice.

And the way he walked, the gentleness of his hands on her skin, the subtle male scent that set her senses whirling...

He wasn't ever going to let loose that control.

Enjoy his lovemaking without asking for more, she advised herself, calling on some common sense to banish the unsettling hunger that ached through her. Enjoy *him* while you can, because it isn't going to last.

She loved him, but he'd never even mentioned the word, never asked for her love—and why should he? He assumed she was sophisticated, mature, sensible—and experienced.

Lying in his house, sprawled between sheets still crumpled from their lovemaking, she saw the future as clearly as if she were clairvoyant. They would remain lovers for...oh, for six months or so, possibly even a year or two, then slowly he'd become tired of her or meet someone else he wanted more. He'd expect a civilised ending to their affair; they'd agree it was over and they'd remain friends.

Pain shafted through her, so acute she froze and hardly dared to breathe.

It would kill her. She flung an arm up to shield her eyes, but caught sight of the time on the bedside clock.

'Nine o'clock!' she gasped, and leapt out of bed.

Fifteen busy minutes later, she was walking out of her room. The wild-haired woman she'd seen in the mirror was replaced by a carefully coiffed, sleekly made-up, self-reliant princess whose only betraying feature was a mouth slightly more full than it had been yesterday.

She hoped the mask hid the turmoil inside her. Making love with Alex had been heart-shakingly wonderful, so why on earth was she nervous at the thought of seeing him again?

Her pulse jumped wildly when a door down the corridor opened and he strode out. His frown dissipated a little when he saw her, but she sensed that wall of inherent reserve implacably back in place.

Her mouth dried. He looked no different. A cynical voice inside her head asked, *Why would he? He's not in love.*

'You should have woken me,' she said, colouring when she realised the implications of her words. Rapidly, she added, 'I didn't intend to sleep in.'

Although he smiled, his eyes were watchful. 'You needed it.' He dropped a swift, almost impersonal kiss on her cheek.

Serina had to stop herself from reaching up to him.

When he straightened his eyes were narrowed and intent and he said softly, 'Another morning I'll enjoy waking you, but this time I thought it best to let you sleep. Now you're up, come and have some breakfast.'

Fighting back a niggling disappointment, Serina went with him. What had she expected him to do? Sweep her into his arms and kiss her passionately there in the corridor, where the housekeeper might walk past at any minute?

Not Alex's style, she thought with a secret grimace, and not hers either.

But some slightly more significant acknowledgement of their rapturous time together would be—well, *comforting.*

Serina thought she'd be unable to eat anything, but

once in the sunny breakfast room she discovered an appetite. Coffee helped too.

And so did the news that Alex had contacted a couple of gardeners who were happy to let her look over their domains. 'Although,' he added, 'they wanted a month or so to prepare them.'

She had to laugh. 'And when we go to their gardens they'll tell us it looked superb a week ago, or will look magnificent in another week, but unfortunately it's not quite perfect right now.'

'I see you know the breed,' he said dryly. 'I suggested we go tomorrow. You said you'd need at least three hours in each garden and then you'd want to do an interview afterwards, so I've organised a morning appointment and an afternoon one, and in between we can have lunch. I know a good restaurant not too far from the first garden.'

A certain glint in his eyes warmed her. 'That sounds very pleasant,' she said demurely.

Building high romantic hopes and castles in the air would be foolish, a sure recipe for a broken heart. She couldn't afford to expect more from this liaison than he'd offered.

Love hadn't been a part of their unspoken agreement. Alex had made it obvious he wanted her, and for her own reasons—delicious, dangerous, but irresistible—she'd decided he should be the man to initiate her into the delights of sex.

Good instincts—she'd made an excellent choice, she told herself stoutly. Inspired, even; Alex was everything a first lover should be.

She hoped he hadn't found her wanting in any way...
Too late to worry about that now.

And, to fill in the silence between them, she embarked on the sort of inconsequential chat she knew so well.

Alex's raised brows showed her that he knew what she was doing—possibly even why—but he responded. Slowly her tension evaporated and somehow, without being aware of how it happened, she found herself talking about her brother.

'He was my father's favourite,' she said without rancour. 'For years Papa was sure he'd be able to return to Montevel, and I'm afraid Doran was brought up to believe it was a possibility. Then, when Doran was about fourteen, Papa finally accepted it was not, and for some reason he more or less ignored Doran after that.'

Alex looked surprised. 'Why?'

Carefully keeping a futile anger from her words, she said, 'I think he could only see Doran as a prospective king. Once he finally accepted there was no longer a throne—and never would be—to inherit, Papa lost interest in him.'

'You're describing a rather grotesquely self-centred man,' Alex said austerely.

'I know. I'm afraid Papa was.' It still hurt to remember how Doran had tried to win his father's attention in any way he could, and his despair and anger when he realised it was no use.

Aware of Alex's scrutiny, she said quietly, 'It's almost as though Papa felt that our family's only value was to produce rulers of Montevel. So when he accepted that Doran was never going to be King, it meant we were worthless.'

Alex frowned. 'How did your father treat you?'

'The same way he treated all women,' she said lightly. 'With compliments—whether earned or not—on my

beauty and an expectation that I would forgive him anything because of who he was.'

Startled, she stopped. Confiding her family's dynam-
ics was not a conversational topic she'd ever indulged in
before—and to Alex, of all people!

Hardly sophisticated behaviour on her part. She said
dismissively, 'He was an excellent father in many ways,
and it's too late to wish he'd treated Doran differently.'

Alex let her steer the conversation towards New
Zealand's native plants—about which he was very
knowledgeable. Serina allowed herself to think it gave
them something else in common.

Something apart from wild passion, she thought, her
skin heating as a stray memory barged into her brain.

'That is a very fetching blush,' Alex said softly.

Their gazes met, lingered, and he reached across the
table and carried her hand to his lips. Little rills of excitement zinged through her at the touch of his mouth
on her palm, and her breath came quickly.

'I have a bach,' he said and smiled at her incompre-
hension. 'That's what North Islanders call small beach
houses.'

'Do you have dialects?' she asked in astonishment.

'No, just the occasional different word. South Islanders
use the word crib to describe the same thing. The Maori
language has dialects, although it's mutually intelligible
right through the country—and through the parts of the
Pacific colonised by Polynesians. My bach is beside one
of the prettiest beaches on the station. Would you like to
spend some time with me there?'

When she hesitated, he added, 'It's not far away, so
we can go out each day to check up on gardens.'

And they'd be private—no chance of Lindy Harcourt

interrupting. Uncertainly, Serina asked, 'Can you afford the time?'

'I'll be in contact if I need to be. The bach is set up for communications.'

So she'd be able to keep in touch with Doran—not, she thought wryly, that he was missing her at all. She looked across the table, thrilled at the impact of cool blue eyes, and made up her mind. 'Yes, thank you, it sounds lovely.'

'I don't think lovely,' she said wryly when they arrived at the bach, 'was exactly the right word.'

Alex looked at her. 'So what is the right word?'

'If I were writing about this I'd use breathtaking,' she told him, her stunned glance travelling along a beach of amber sand, curved like a slice of melon between headlands made sombre by the huge silver-edged domes of trees she knew were called pohutukawas.

'And as you're not writing about it?' he said coolly, unloading the Land Rover.

She stiffened, then shrugged, some of her delight in the cove evaporating. 'Breathtaking still does it for me,' she said lightly, reaching for a refrigerated box.

'That's too heavy for you,' Alex said, handing her a bag of groceries. 'Take this.'

Packing the contents away would take her mind off his casual strength as he hefted her case and the box of food out of the Land Rover.

The bach was larger than she'd imagined and extremely comfortable, furnished in a style that breathed a sophisticated beachside ambience. It certainly didn't lack amenities.

As she looked up from a swift inspection of the kitchen he asked, 'Can you cook?'

Her brows shot up. 'Of course. Can you?'

'Several dishes extremely well, scrambled eggs being my forte. And I can do labouring stuff like peeling potatoes. Where did you learn?'

'I took lessons.'

'While you were at finishing school?' His voice was satiric.

'No,' she said quietly. 'After my parents died. When Doran came home during the holidays I realised I'd have to do better than the few meals and techniques I'd mastered, so I learnt how. My godmother paid for the course.'

He said, 'Losing your parents must have been tough.'

'Yes.' She added, 'But you lost your mother early so you know what it's like. At least I had mine for longer.'

To her astonishment, he came and pulled her into his arms. She stiffened, but he held her close and because there was nothing sexual in his embrace she relaxed, taking comfort from the solid thump of his heart and the warmth of his body.

He said quietly, 'There are several bedrooms here. Do you want a room to yourself?'

Stunned, Serina kept her head down. How to deal with this? With courage, she told herself.

She looked up into narrowed gleaming eyes. 'No,' she said, heart thumping erratically. 'I don't need a room to myself.'

Four days later Serina woke early, her head pillowed on Alex's shoulder, and faced the stark fact that she'd made the wrong decision. Coming to the bach with Alex had been more than a mistake—it had been stupid. It would have been far safer to stay at the homestead, where the housekeeper was a sort of chaperone, someone to make sure emotions didn't run riot.

Alone here with him, Serina had fallen deeper and deeper in love, become happier than she'd ever been in her life.

Lax after a strenuous night's loving, completely adjusted to the sleek strength of his body against hers, she had never felt so secure.

The past days had been...

She searched for the right word to describe them, but for once her mind failed her. Her life before Alex seemed faded and dim, like an old photograph left in the sun too long. With him, everything was more vivid, her emotions infinitely more intense, her physical reactions richer, so that the colours of the world around her almost hurt her eyes.

Even food tasted better, she thought, amused by the thought.

But then that could be because Alex's scrambled eggs were superb.

And he was certainly appreciative of the simple French country cuisine she knew so well. He enjoyed helping, too. A smile curled her lips as she recalled his expertise with a potato peeler.

Carefully still, she lay soaking up the quiet delight of these moments. The muted hush of wavelets on the glowing sand made a serene background to the quiet sound of his breathing.

She glanced up at his sleeping face, her eyes caressing the uncompromising sweep of cheekbones, the blade of his nose, the compelling forcefulness of the features that would keep him a handsome man all his life.

Her heart contracted and she fought back the desire to reach out and touch him, reassure herself that she was truly with him. Loving Alex had added a different dimension to her life.

For as long as it lasted.

Wincing, she urged her thoughts in a less painful direction. These past days he'd taken her to small gardens and large ones, gardens overlooking the sea and gardens high in the hills that ran up the central spine of Northland's narrow peninsula.

Some of the houses had been intensely luxurious, their owners clearly wealthy folk who employed gardeners to take care of extensive grounds; other owners lived in comfortable farmhouses and did all their own work. A couple of cottages had been almost spartan in their simplicity, but without fail every owner had been hospitable and pleasant, eager to show off their hard work and the driving inspiration that had led to their superb gardens.

Because of Alex. They all knew him, admired him and responded in their various ways to his inbuilt authority.

The previous morning they'd visited a particularly idiosyncratic garden overlooking a long white beach. Native shrubs had clothed the hills around, and in their shelter a middle-aged woman with an eye for amazing colour combinations had made herself a stunning garden, assisted by a husband wryly resigned to ever more of his farm being co-opted as she dreamed up new schemes. A passionate follower of growing organically, their hostess produced her own vegetables and tended an orchard filled with fruits Serina had never seen before.

It had been fascinating and fun; the couple knew Alex well, and the warmth of their welcome was genuine and open.

As well, they had an enchanting granddaughter, a solemn little girl of about six called Nora, who shyly showed Serina her favourite places in the garden and, when she realised Serina could speak a different language, begged to be taught a French song. They'd spent a laughing ten minutes while she learned a simple nursery rhyme under the indulgent eyes of Alex and her grandparents.

After that Nora had stuck close to Serina, watching as she took photographs and having to be coaxed to go with her grandfather and Alex to see some new calves when Serina had settled down in the sun to interview the owner.

That too went off extremely well and their hostess insisted on them staying for lunch, a superb spread she'd cooked herself.

As they drank coffee afterwards, Nora edged up to Serina and said, 'Grandma said you're a princess. Why aren't you wearing your crown?'

'Nora!' her grandmother said swiftly. 'Darling, that's not very polite.'

Serina said, 'It's all right. I expect Nora's seen a lot of pictures of princesses with crowns. But princesses only look like princesses when they're wearing their crowns. Once they take them off, they're just ordinary people.'

Nora frowned. 'In my fav'rite book Princess Polly wears her crown even when she's riding her pony.'

'Ah, but that's in a book,' Serina said. 'And I'm not really a princess because you have to belong to a country to be a true princess, and I don't.'

Nora considered that, then said, 'You could belong to us.'

Touched, Serina said, 'Even if I did, I wouldn't wear a crown very much. They only come out for special occasions—like balls and big parties. They're like high-heeled shoes—you don't wear them when you go to visit friends, or lovely gardens like your grandma's.' She leaned forward and lowered her voice. 'Actually, they're quite heavy.'

Nora's eyes widened and a thought struck her. 'Well, if you married Uncle Alex you could be *our* princess and then you could wear your crown when you came here, couldn't you?'

Colour burned a trail along Serina's cheekbones. What on earth could she say to that—certainly not that it was something she didn't dare hope for!

Alex said, 'Serina lives on the other side of the world, Nora. She might be wanting to marry someone there.'

Serina managed a laugh. 'Not right at this moment,' she said and smiled down at Nora, whose face had fallen. 'Before we go, why don't you write out your name and address on a piece of paper and give it to me? When I get home I'll send you a postcard of the place I live. It's very beautiful, but quite different from here.'

Nora's face brightened but she said seriously, 'You could come and see us a lot if you married Uncle Alex.'

Alex interposed smoothly, 'How would it be if Princess Serina sent you a photo of herself wearing her crown?'

After a moment's hesitation and a glance at her grandmother, Nora clearly recalled her manners. 'Yes, thank you,' she said unconvincingly.

Recalling the conversation now, Serina's skin burned again. Until the little girl's artless suggestion, she hadn't even considered marriage—and she wasn't going to consider it now, she told herself sternly.

Because it was never going to happen.

But, in spite of her resolution, she allowed herself a moment or two of imagining herself walking down the aisle on Doran's arm towards Alex…picturing happy domesticity with perhaps a little girl like Nora one day.

He'd been good with the child, and Nora clearly loved him.

Stupid, she scolded and ruthlessly banished the fantasy, ignoring the bleak ache in her heart and concentrated on how nice the New Zealanders she'd met had been…

From outside a seagull called, its harsh screech overriding the muted hush of the waves only a few steps from the bach. Alex's breathing altered and the arm about her tightened, but after a moment he relaxed and the regular rhythm of his breaths resumed.

Serina relaxed too, setting her mind to assess whatever it was about him that had made her fall so far and so headlong into love.

Nice was the last word she'd use for him—it was far too pallid a description of his keen mind and charged energy, a word totally unable to convey the authority with which he harnessed both attributes to an iron-clad will.

As for the particular sexual charisma that made him stand out in any crowd…

She gave a voluptuous little wriggle. Without opening his eyes, Alex said, 'No.'

'No what?' she asked cautiously.

'No to anything.' He lifted lashes that were unfairly long for a man and skewered her with a long considering stare. 'I'm exhausted.'

Serina pretended belief. 'In that case, I suppose we'd better get up.'

'Mmm,' he murmured and clamped her more closely to his side. 'How many more gardeners did I misguidedly contact for you?'

'Seven,' she returned promptly. 'Why misguidedly? That was the whole purpose of my visit, remember.'

In one swift movement that took her by surprise, Alex turned and pinned her underneath him. He certainly didn't *feel* exhausted, she decided, her body responding with unrestrained eagerness.

'Because, if it weren't for all those phone calls, we could be spending the day in bed together,' he said calmly and kissed her.

When she melted beneath him, already hot and yielding, he lifted his head so his breath fanned across the tender curves of her lips in a way that made her wriggle again.

Breaking the kiss, he murmured, 'So I suppose we'd better get up and sally forth.'

'You dare,' she breathed, linking her hands across his back and narrowing her eyes.

He laughed, challenge glinting blue and brilliant in his eyes. 'How are you going to stop me?' he said, and startled her by turning onto his side, and then onto his back so he could gaze up at the ceiling.

Serina absorbed the arrogant lines of his profile

against the sunlight outside. 'I'm not going to,' she said demurely. 'If you're exhausted you'd be no use to me anyway.'

'Of no use to you?' he said in a tone that made her instinctively try to sit up.

He forestalled her by stretching a languid arm across her waist—languid until she tried a little harder, when it turned to steel and pinioned her to the bed.

'Let's see, shall we?' he said thoughtfully, and turned to face her again.

Her breath blocked her throat and she surrendered to the slow glide of a hand from her throat, across her breasts and onwards, inching by painfully exciting increments to that certain spot between her thighs where he knew a welcome awaited him.

Held a willing prisoner, she sneaked a seething glance from half-closed eyes. His expression a mixture of amusement and lust, he was clearly enjoying his sensuous exploration, his fingers brushing at the satin skin, tracing an old scar.

'What was this?'

'Appendix,' she said vaguely as those tormenting, tantalising fingers drifted closer…closer…closer…

Heat burned through her and her wilful body arced off the sheet.

Alex looked down at her with a wicked gleam. 'Useless?' he enquired, and let his hand drift back up to her breasts. 'It's unusual for anyone to have their appendix out nowadays.'

'It wasn't nowadays.'

'How old were you?'

'Six. My father believed that a grumbling appendix should always be removed—his grandmother had died from appendicitis.' Serina's voice sounded vague and fluttery, the words jumping out unevenly as her breath came in swift pants.

Alex bent his head. Her breasts had already peaked, the small aureoles standing proud and expectant, eager for the warm stimulation of his mouth.

But, to her astonishment and intense frustration, he kissed the scar.

'What—?' she muttered.

The imperative summons of a cellphone jerked her out of the sensuous haze he'd summoned so swiftly.

Alex said something under his breath and got out of bed to pick it up. Gaze fixed on her face, he barked, 'Yes?'

Serina lay still, intent on the way the morning sun glowed on his bronze skin, turning it gold, picking out the swell of each muscle, the long powerful lines of his torso and legs.

An alteration in his tone whipped her attention back to his face. It had set like stone and the heat had vanished from his eyes, leaving them hard and cold.

'When?' he demanded, turning abruptly and striding out of the room.

Serina hauled the sheet over her and listened to his voice in the next room, crisp and decisive, clearly giving orders. A swift fear chilled her.

CHAPTER NINE

SERINA wondered uneasily if she should get up. Judging by the icily formidable tone of Alex's voice, something had gone seriously wrong. But, before she had a chance to move, he came back in and said, grim-faced, 'Your brother has left Vanuatu.'

She sat upright. 'What?'

'You don't know?' He scrutinised her face with a flat, lethal gaze.

She shook her head to clear it, then went to fling back the sheet. 'I'll check my email.'

'In a moment,' Alex said curtly. 'You told me he was having a great time there.'

It sounded too close to an accusation for her to be comfortable.

Spiritedly, she said, 'He is—was. But he's always been impulsive—and I've been surprised his passion for diving has lasted so long. I think I told you that. He probably got tired of the heat, or there weren't enough pretty girls there to flirt with...'

Her voice trailed away under Alex's cold, uncompromising survey. This was a man she didn't know—but one whose existence she'd always suspected. No longer a lover, he was the ruthless warrior she'd sensed beneath the cool sophistication.

He said sternly, 'Serina, if you value your brother's life and safety, tell me everything—*anything*—you know about this so-called game he's been involved with.'

Bewildered, she said, 'I've already told you.'

'Not enough.'

Panic kicked beneath her ribs and she demanded urgently, 'What is going on? Why should you be so concerned about Doran leaving Vanuatu, and what *is* it about that stupid computer game?'

'Because he's heading for the border region between Carathia and Montevel, and the game you've been so blithely unconcerned about is no video fake; it's for real.'

Serina stared at him, reacting with a pang of fear to the uncompromising conviction in his expression. 'Don't be silly,' she said, but half-heartedly. 'What do you mean—for real?'

'This is no joke. Face it. You've been fed a fairy tale—a very clever fairy tale—to keep you quiet while Doran, his friends and several others finalised their plans to foment a popular uprising in Montevel in the hope that they'll eventually be able to take over the country.'

Stomach clenching as though to ward off a blow, she blurted, 'That's ridiculous! It sounds as though someone's been feeding *you*—or Gerd—a fairy tale.'

'No,' he said inflexibly.

Only one word, but it was delivered in a voice that delivered absolute conviction.

Trying to convince herself now as much as him, she said, 'Doran and his friends aren't stupid—why would they think they have any chance of *taking over* Montevel?

They don't have any money—exiled aristocrats don't do terribly well once they have to earn their living, it seems. And none of them have any tactical or military knowledge, or contacts in Montevel or…or anything.' She firmed her voice and said more strongly, 'If that call was from Gerd, he's overreacting. He must be.'

Lethally, Alex said, 'He's not. Your brother and his merry little band of romantic idiots plan to use Carathia's Adriatic coast as a safe haven and jumping-off point. As for money and military knowledge—they have a backer who is providing both.'

Fear forcing adrenalin through her, Serina scrambled out of bed. She glanced down, realised she was naked and yanked the sheet from the bed, winding it around herself. Alex's gaze didn't waver and she realised that, whatever was going on, he believed Gerd's version—if it was Gerd who'd contacted him. She dragged in a breath and tried to persuade her whirling brain to reason logically.

It was too far-fetched—it had to be.

She risked another glance at Alex's stony face and into the turmoil of her fears about her brother there infiltrated a sad little thought that he'd probably invited her out here—perhaps even seduced her—hoping she'd…

Stop it, she told herself. Doran was too important to let her own barely-born, unacknowledged hopes and longings get in the way of his welfare.

Alex was a formidable magnate, used to the ruthless cut and thrust of the business world, and Gerd was another powerful, intelligent man, a ruler who'd fought and won a civil war in the mountains of Carathia.

Neither they—nor their security organisations—were likely to suffer delusions. They must really believe that

Doran planned to use Carathia as a base for some forlorn hope concerning Montevel. And, if that was so, then her brother had deliberately and systematically lied to her. Worse—much worse—than that; he was in terrible danger.

The cold pool beneath her ribs expanded right through her. Numbly, she said, 'Alex, are you sure?'

Relentless eyes rebuffed her pleading gaze. 'Completely sure.'

She didn't need the assurance; her own words had already told her that she accepted what he'd said.

She could feel the colour drain from her face. 'I have to go,' she said starkly. 'See if I can talk sense into them.'

'You can't.' Alex's statement sounded unmistakably like a man in charge.

Shivering, she pulled the sheet tighter around her and walked out of the bedroom, coming to a stop by the wall of glass that looked out onto the cove. Although she concentrated fiercely on the view, she could see nothing but blurred colours and shapes.

'So how much do you know about this supposed game?' Alex asked her from behind, his question hammering at her. 'Has he discussed any of the manoeuvres, the twists and turns, the basic plot lines?'

'No.' She squared her shoulders. 'Apart from the vampires,' she added, her voice cracking on the final word. Doran's little joke, obviously. She blinked hard and asked, 'Who is backing them—and why?'

'The less you know, the better.'

Angry, Serina turned to meet his eyes—implacable, so arctic she felt as though they pierced through to her innermost being. There would be no negotiation. She'd been kept in ignorance by him too.

'I don't know anything.' She added bitterly, 'And, as his sister, I don't have enough influence with Doran to persuade him to stop.'

'I didn't imagine you would,' he agreed. 'I wasn't going to suggest it.'

'What are you going to do?'

He said briefly, 'I don't have any official standing at all, so Gerd will deal with it.'

Her lips trembled. 'And he's on his honeymoon. Poor Rosie.'

The knot of panic in her stomach stopped any further words. If anyone could extricate Doran from this, she'd trust Gerd to do it.

But after a moment she said, 'I—I'm just finding it impossible to accept that they thought there was any chance they'd be able to start a revolution. It's—just so *crazy*.'

'They were fed a line,' Alex said curtly. 'By someone unscrupulous enough to use their youth and their innocence against them. Any sort of revolution is damned difficult to get off the ground and, although the current regime there isn't exactly a benign one, it's a lot better than the dictator who booted your grandparents out. And infinitely better than the civil war they endured to get rid of him. Most of the citizens seem happy enough with their present situation.'

He waited and when she said nothing he added harshly, 'If Doran and his cohorts go ahead with this hare-brained plot, people will die.'

Serina clutched at the sheet, huddling into it to stop herself shivering. 'I've been trying to reject the whole idea because I don't *want* to believe it.' She met his formidable blue gaze squarely, knowing she wasn't going to get the reassurance she craved. 'You're sure—utterly and completely sure—that this is not just some student prank that will evaporate into thin air as soon as the practicalities become too much for them to cope with?'

'I'm sure,' he said levelly and not without sympathy. 'As far as I can gather, they're hyped on a mixture of romantic Ruritanian fantasy and a cast-iron conviction that the people of Montevel will welcome them with open arms.'

'Why should they believe that?' she asked despairingly, not expecting an answer.

Cuttingly, Alex said, 'Because they want to, and because they've been told that by someone they trust.'

'Does this—*someone*—have anything to do with the organisation that tried to take over the carathite mines in Carathia a while ago?'

Anxiously, she waited for his answer. A rare and valuable mineral found on the border of Carathia and Montevel, carathite was used in electronics. The crown of Carathia owned the mines and Gerd had been forced to battle his own civil war, one fomented by an unscrupulous firm with its eyes on the mines.

'No. That firm no longer exists, and the men who started that uprising are either dead or in jail. Between us, Gerd and Kelt and I made sure they got their just deserts.'

His ruthless tone lifted the hairs on the back of Serina's neck. Before she could ask another question, he went on, 'I'll tell you this much—if they're who we think they might be, the instigators aren't in the least interested in Gerd or any possibility of carathite being found in Montevel.' He paused, giving weight to his next words. 'They're possibly using your brother's rebellion as a diversion.'

Horrified, she stared at him. Although her lips formed the word *Why?*, no sound emerged.

Alex read her correctly. 'Right now, the reason doesn't matter. I just wanted to make sure you knew how serious this is.'

'You're trying to frighten me,' she said numbly.

He didn't soften. 'I hope I'm succeeding.'

'Oh, you are,' she said bleakly. 'What...do you know what Doran is planning to do?'

'I suspect the plan is to sail to Montevel in a hired yacht and slip ashore once they've made landfall.'

She swallowed. 'I see.' She shivered again, but said fiercely, 'I want to go home.'

'No.'

She said curtly, 'Alex, I can't stay here without trying to do something.'

'You can,' he said with calm authority. 'Because there is nothing you can do, and you're safe here.'

'I might be able to convince Doran—'

'You said yourself you have no influence on him,' he reminded her implacably. 'How are you going to get back?'

'I'll fly, of course—' She stopped abruptly because she didn't have the money to get her halfway round the world.

One glance at his saturnine face told her she wasn't going to persuade him to provide her with the jet he shared with his cousins.

Never mind; her credit card would get her there, and somehow she'd pay it off.

'Alex, he's my *brother*. I have to do what I can.'

Alex could see that the words were wrung from her. She knew how unlikely it was that she'd be able to do anything to stop this mad scheme of Doran's, but she wanted to be as close to her brother as she could be.

He didn't blame her. What she didn't know was that if Doran was killed, she could well be next on the list. She was the last member of the royal family there, and while alive she would be a constant focus for any dissatisfaction.

But, even if he told her that, he suspected she'd go anyway.

So he said bluntly, 'It's not a good idea.'

She met his eyes with a level, determined look that warned him she refused to be intimidated. 'Perhaps not, but I'm going just the same. I'll ring the airline.'

'Princess, you're not going anywhere.'

Mouth drying, she stared at him, her heart thumping with heavy emphasis. 'You can't stop me,' she challenged starkly. 'You might be lord of all you survey here, but you have no power over me.'

'I can prevent you from leaving New Zealand,' he said coolly, 'and I plan to do just that.'

'How? I hope you don't think that your prowess in bed is enough to dazzle me into submission?'

He showed his teeth in a smile that pulled every tiny hair on her body upright. 'That has nothing to do with this.'

'Then you'll have to be a jailer,' she flung at him furiously.

'Serina, you're not going anywhere near this mess. You'll stay out of danger if I have to chain you to the bed to keep you here.'

The ruthless note in his voice made her shiver. She stared mutely at him, wrenched by anger and terror for her brother. She wanted nothing more than to have Alex take her in his arms and tell her that everything would be all right, that Doran was safe and that the whole thing had been an elaborate hoax, a joke…

In a slightly more gentle voice, Alex said, 'I suggest you get dressed and see if Doran has left any message for you.'

Serina started. 'Oh—yes. I'll do it right now. If you'll excuse me, I'll put some clothes on,' she said evenly.

He paused, his gaze speculative, then nodded. Stomach churning, Serina dashed into the bedroom and hauled her laptop from its case. While it fired up, she pulled on her wrap and pushed her tangled hair back from her face, urging the computer to hurry up, still gripped by a cold, sick panic.

Doran had sent her two lines.

Don't worry, everything's going to be fine. I'll see you soon.

Hastily, she fired off a message in return. *Don't do anything*, she wrote, fingers shaking so much she had to stop and clench her hands for a moment before she could tell him their plans had been discovered.

She jumped, quivering with shock when a hand reached over her and deleted her words. Unable to bear the fear scything through her, she froze as Alex closed down her computer.

'I can't let you send it,' he said tersely. 'The only safety he has is that we have some idea of what's going to happen. If they realise they've been rumbled, God knows what they might do.'

She asked dully, 'How do you know their plans?'

'They set the whole scheme up like a video game,' he told her. 'My men have managed to hack into one computer.'

Hope whispered through her. 'Then how do you know it's not just a game?'

'One of my men infiltrated the group. Stop grasping at straws, Serina. It's not a game. It's deadly serious.'

Stumbling, she got to her feet and Alex turned her into his arms and held her, enveloping her in the heat of his body.

She said fiercely, 'I could kill him, the idiot.' Then caught her breath, horrified by the tumbling words.

'It's all right,' Alex said quietly.

But she shook her head. 'Where is he?'

'He's still in flight.'

'Where to?'

'He's landing in Rome,' he told her.

Stiffly, aching as though she'd been beaten, she pulled away from the unexpected comfort of his arms. 'I need a shower.'

'I'll make breakfast.' And, when she opened her mouth to say she couldn't swallow anything, he said bluntly, 'Starving yourself is not going to help either Doran or you.'

Serina gathered her clothes and walked into the bathroom. She was already under the water when she thought savagely that he clearly didn't expect her to climb out of a window and flee.

No doubt because he knew very well she had no way of working out how to travel cross-country back to the homestead. And, as she had no idea where he kept the keys to the Land Rover, she couldn't steal that and drive out.

But she had to get back…

Her passport and credit card were in her bag.

Leaving the shower on, she scrambled out, grabbing a towel to blot off some water as she headed towards the door.

Scrabbling in her bag revealed that neither passport nor credit card were there any longer. Her terror gave way to outrage when she realised Alex had also taken her cellphone. Furious, she stormed through to the kitchen and confronted him.

'Give them back to me!' she commanded. 'Right now, or I'll—I'll…'

With intensely infuriating control, he said, 'You'll get everything back when you leave New Zealand.'

Serina stared at him, her anger almost boiling over, and realised he hadn't responded in any way to her semi-nakedness.

With stark pain, she accepted that he'd got her here, lured her into his arms, into his bed, made love to her with heart-stopping passion, brought her to the bach—all to coax what information he could from her.

She'd never felt so helpless, so utterly without resources. So completely at someone else's mercy. So blazingly angry.

So wrenchingly unhappy…

It took every last ounce of fortitude she possessed to say grittily, 'I despise you.'

Without waiting for any answer, she turned and stumbled blindly back into the bathroom. Frustration and grief churning through her, she lifted her face to the showerhead, trying to wash away her fear for her brother, her anger with Alex and a frozen, bitter anguish because he'd used her.

A knock on the door made her start and turn off the water.

Through the door, Alex asked, 'Are you all right?'

'Yes,' she called, a little warmed by his thoughtfulness. Surely…surely it hadn't just been a cold-blooded seduction?

She stepped out of the shower, slicking her wet hair back from her face and started to dry herself. Face facts, Serina, she thought starkly.

Alex and Gerd must have decided to get her and Doran out of the way in the hope that this would stop the group from going ahead with their plans. Which meant that, however thoughtful he was, however great a lover, Alex's seduction had been a deliberate ploy, a subterfuge to keep her out of the way while he and Gerd tried to find out what Doran's group were plotting.

Shattered by just how much that thought hurt, she hastily got into her clothes and combed her hair straight back from her face, lecturing herself all the time.

Love was transient; she knew that. People had their hearts broken on a regular basis; they wept, they suffered, they told the tabloids all about it and then, six months later, they were happily in love with someone else.

She'd get over it.

Another tap on the bathroom door had her whirling around. No, she thought in panic, she wasn't ready…

Uncannily echoing her thoughts, Alex said, 'Breakfast's ready.'

She hadn't blow-dried her hair or applied any cosmetics. She stared at her reflection, then gave a quick shrug. It no longer mattered. If he couldn't cope with the real Serina she didn't care.

But deep down—so deep she could almost bury

it—lurked a painful understanding that Alex was the only man she would ever love like this, the only one able to hold her heart in his keeping.

Even though he didn't want it.

Five minutes later, a bleak smile curved her mouth when she realised he had scrambled eggs for them both, grilled tomatoes and made toast.

He examined her face. 'You look pale,' he said abruptly.

'It's not every day I'm told I'm a prisoner. I dare say I'll get used to it.'

He gave her a hard, sardonic smile. 'You manage to look ravishing in spite of it,' he told her, bringing a wash of colour to her skin as he surveyed her. 'And coffee will probably give you some colour.'

He set a plate in front of her and, in spite of her anger and her fear for Doran, her stomach growled. 'Thank you,' she said stiffly and picked up her utensils.

The food put new heart into her; although she couldn't eat everything he'd piled on the plate, she made good inroads into it. Pride kept her shoulders straight, her eyes level, her voice cool and uninflected.

And coffee helped. After pouring herself a large mug, she said, 'What do you think Doran will do once he reaches Rome?'

'I suspect he'll be picked up by someone from the conspiracy and taken by boat to a safe place inside Carathia—a port town. From there, they'll probably island-hop to somewhere on Montevel's coast in a yacht.'

She set her mug down with a small crash. 'They're mad! How on earth do they think they're going to topple the rulers there—a group of university kids with more brains than sense?'

'They're expecting the populace to rise up with them once they've been given a leader.'

'Doran,' she said numbly.

'Yes—and it just might work. To people who've had a pretty rough time for the past fifty years, the idea of the King returning and bringing good times with him could be potent enough to start an uprising.'

'But the rulers control the military,' she said, her voice dragging.

He nodded. 'Exactly—although even the forces have been restive lately. Their pay has been cut and a very popular general was court-martialled and shot by firing squad for mutiny.'

Serina picked up the coffee cup, noting with an odd detachment that her hand was trembling. She finally managed to drink the rest of the liquid down before asking a question that had been bothering her.

'Why is Gerd so concerned about this? It's really nothing to do with him—and, anyway, I'd have thought he'd be happy with a less repressive regime on his doorstep.'

'The last time Montevel suffered a revolt Carathia had to deal with about fifty thousand refugees,' Alex told her bluntly.

'I see,' she said, startled by the number. 'I hadn't even thought about that.'

'And unrest along the borders makes every ruler uneasy.' He glanced at his watch. 'Right, are you ready to go?'

His words made no sense. She stared at him and he elaborated, 'We're looking at gardens, Serina.'

'I couldn't,' she said involuntarily, stunned that he should expect her to carry on as though nothing had happened.

He shrugged. 'I'd have thought it a much better way to deal with the situation than sitting here anguishing over it.'

At that moment she hated him. 'This is my *brother* we're talking about,' she said between her teeth.

'So you're going to sit here and worry without being able to do a thing to affect the outcome?' he returned, coolly challenging.

She glared at him. 'I thought I was a prisoner here.'

'A prisoner, yes, if you want to think of yourself like that,' he agreed calmly. 'Not necessarily confined to one place, though.'

Serina got to her feet. Which didn't make much of a difference to the intimidation factor—he still towered over her. Tonelessly, she said, 'All right, I'll go.'

It was a strange day. She managed to behave normally—smiling, making polite conversation to both garden owners, conducting the interviews with something of her usual concentration. Stony professional pride drove her to compose her photographs with as much care as usual.

But she felt as though she'd been sliced in two; no, she thought on the way home, in three. One part was the magazine columnist, the other the sister anguishing over her brother, and the final part the lover coping with betrayal.

When at last they drove up to the bach, she barely waited for the Land Rover to stop before bolting out.

Alex watched her run into the bach and followed

her. She'd done well, but for the whole day he'd felt the barriers firmly in place.

As though she blamed him for this whole situation, even though it had been caused by her brother. Damn the kid—if he weren't heading straight towards death, Alex would have carpeted him, amongst other things pointing out just how much his actions upset his sister.

And some part of him was angry with Serina for being so intransigent. He'd expected her to want to go to Carathia; what he hadn't expected was his exasperation and anger at her flinty resistance to him.

Once inside, he said, 'I'll make you some tea while you write up your notes.'

She swallowed and flashed him a stunned glance, then seemed to shrink. 'Thank you,' she said quietly.

Writing up her notes by hand took up the rest of the afternoon. After a meal she didn't taste, she said, 'I'd like to watch the news on television.'

He switched on the set and joined her on the sofa. Tension tore at her—not the exciting, sensuous tension of the previous days, but a feeling that was rooted in pain.

Gradually—so gradually she hadn't really realised what was happening—she'd learned to trust Alex. That cautious, hard-won faith lay in shards around her now.

Without taking much in, she watched the parade across the screen of statesmen and politicians, celebrities and unfortunates whose lives had somehow become camera fodder.

Nothing about Montevel...

When it was over, Alex said, 'Is there anything else you want to watch?'

'No, thanks.'

'In that case, I suggest you go to bed.'

She glanced at her watch. 'It's barely eight o'clock.'

'Neither of us got much sleep last night.'

She flinched, memories flooding back of the previous night's passion. Scrambling to her feet, she said stiffly, 'I'll make up a bed in the other bedroom.'

'No.'

Her head came up and she eyed him with frozen composure. If she had to spend the night in his bed something inside her would die, she thought fiercely. 'I am not sleeping with you.'

He got to his feet, lithe and big and completely determined. 'I can't force you to sleep, of course, but you're spending the night in my bed.'

His cool insistence goaded her into saying, 'I give you my word I won't try to run away.'

'Good, but that doesn't change anything,' he said, his tone telling her there was no option. 'I won't expect sex, if that's what's worrying you.'

White-lipped, she said, 'You can't—*won't*—force me to sleep with you, surely.'

His eyes narrowed as he said softly, 'Of course I wouldn't, Princess.'

Her composure cracked. Hands clenched by her sides, she snapped, 'Don't call me that! How would you feel if I called you Businessman all the time?'

'Irritated,' he conceded, a glimmer of amusement in the blue ice of his eyes shattering what was left of her precarious poise.

'You might think it's funny, but I find it demeaning and insulting and completely infuriating, and I'm sick and tired of it and I want you to stop.' She stopped, biting back the even more intemperate words that jostled for freedom in her brain.

'Very well, I won't do it again. Now, get ready for bed.'

They measured gazes like duellers. Then she said savagely, 'At least you can't force me to enjoy sleeping with you.'

'I could,' he said with cool, threatening insolence, 'but I'm not going to.'

Serina whirled and stormed into the bedroom, hauling off her clothes with a carelessness that should have shocked her. She crawled into the bed, turned on her side and lay still and fuming, waiting for him to come.

CHAPTER TEN

TRY as she did, Serina couldn't fall sleep before Alex came in. Frantic thoughts jostled in her brain, drowning out the voice of reason that told her she was transferring her anguish and anger to Alex because she couldn't vent it on Doran.

And it was less painful to be furious with Doran than lie there terrified he might be killed.

Eyes clamped shut, she heard Alex come in and the small sounds that indicated he was undressing. Her already rigid body stiffened even further when he slid into the bed beside her.

He didn't touch her. Humiliatingly, her anger dissipated in a flood of bitter, aching regret for the pleasure they'd taken from each other, the joy of discovering how desire enriched her life...

Except that the hours spent in his arms had almost certainly been a means to an end.

And it didn't help that she almost understood his motivation. She would do anything for her brother; it was entirely understandable that Alex should do what he could to help Gerd and Rosie...

Every muscle strained and taut, she fought the urge to turn over. She could hear Alex breathing—steady, relaxed—and decided she hated him. Hot tears squeezed through her lashes; she refused to humiliate herself by giving in to them.

'Go to sleep, Serina,' Alex said lazily.

She couldn't trust her voice enough to give an answer. Eventually, she did sleep, only to wake in the grip of the nightmare. Only this time she was held firmly against Alex and he was saying, 'It's all right, sweetheart. Go back to sleep now.'

But when she woke in the morning she was alone in the bed. It had been a dream, she thought in confusion—a deceiving, treacherous dream, especially the part where he'd held her close to his solid warmth and strength and called her *sweetheart*...

Did he regret their affair, deciding he'd wasted time making love to her when she knew nothing—had been totally taken in by the video game fabrication Doran and his friends had fed her?

Limbs heavy and weighted, she climbed out of the bed and showered, getting into jeans and a T-shirt. It took all of her will to get herself through the bedroom door, but the need to know if Alex had learned anything more about Doran's movements drove her out.

Alex didn't look as though he'd spent a difficult night. He was standing outside in the crisp winter sunlight, talking into a mobile phone, his brows drawn together, but he swung around as soon as she came out.

'All right, then,' he said concisely, snapped the telephone shut and examined her critically. 'All right?'

'Fine, thank you,' she said automatically.

'Doran has managed to evade surveillance,' he said succinctly. 'He hasn't been seen since he left the airport at Rome, but I imagine he's already sailing across the

Adriatic towards Carathia. Gerd's got his coastguard on full alert.'

Alex's voice was neutral, but she turned away from his intent scrutiny. 'So we just have to wait.' And pray, she thought bleakly.

'I'm afraid so.' The leashed impatience she detected in his tone indicated he wasn't accustomed to waiting.

She knew the feeling well, she thought bleakly. Impetuously, she demanded, 'Why won't you tell me who is backing them? Doran hasn't got the money to fly all around the world.'

'Because we still don't know exactly who is producing this show. It could be one of two organisations.' He glanced at his watch. 'Breakfast,' he said curtly. 'And then we'll get on the road.'

She bit back her protest. Staying here, or going back to the homestead to worry the day away wasn't sensible.

That day and the following one were repetitions of the first. Almost sick with worry, Serina plodded doggedly on with her schedule, reluctantly grateful to Alex, who supported her unobtrusively.

Jailer he might be, but he was always there.

Even in bed, she thought on the third morning after Doran's bombshell. She'd woken thinking she was once more in his arms, only to find it was another dream…

Once more he'd left her alone; she got up and dragged herself through her morning routine.

Her heart stopped when she heard Alex call. Still in her pyjamas, she raced through the door, almost colliding with him.

'What?' she gasped, staring up into his face. 'What news?'

'Gerd's security men picked up Doran and several others off the coast of Carathia.'

So relieved she couldn't speak, she felt tears start to her eyes. His arm came around her shoulders. Steadfastly resisting the temptation to sink against him, use his strength to bolster her own, Serina pulled away and finally managed to breathe, 'Thank God.'

'Indeed,' Alex agreed dryly, stepping back.

'He's all right?'

'He's fine, although he's refusing to believe just how close he came to killing not only himself, but all his friends and probably thousands of others too.'

'Is there a way of contacting him?'

'Once Gerd's security men have finished with him, he'll be free to go home, where you can try to make him aware of how dangerously he's been playing.'

She firmed her trembling lips, so awash with conflicting emotions she found it difficult to think. 'Then I'll go home too,' she said swiftly.

He said calmly, 'All right.'

'I'm not asking permission,' she flashed.

His brows lifted, but he said mildly enough, 'I wasn't granting it. I know how you feel—you want to lash out at Doran. It would be a lot more sensible to hurl your feelings at me.'

But she'd regained control of her temper. 'I don't blame you for anything,' she said as calmly as she could.

Only for stealing my heart...

And that was over-dramatising. Hearts stayed firmly lodged in their owners' chests. They might crack or break, but they mended. This pain, the dragging anguish, would ease.

It had to, because she couldn't bear much more of it.

Alex said, 'Doran is going to be acutely defensive; if I can give you some advice, treat him as an adult who's made a mistake and has learned from it. Although I'd point out the inadvisability of lying to those who love him.'

Of course he hadn't meant that to hurt. He didn't know she loved him. Quietly, she said, 'I just hope that he realises once and for all that he has no hope of going back to Montevel.'

'So does everyone,' Alex said austerely. 'He's caused enough trouble—and I'm sure Gerd has made that more than clear to him. If he's got any sense, he'll apply himself to his final year at university and find a career that will keep him busy.'

She asked tentatively, 'Are you going to hold him to working off his plane flights?'

'I am,' Alex said uncompromisingly.

And, during the long journey back to France, she hugged that promise to her heart. It was foolish, of course, but it offered her some comfort at a time when she needed it. If Alex kept in touch, they might…

No, she thought, inserting the key into the lock of her apartment. Don't even think of it. It's not going to happen. This time next year you'll have difficulty remembering Alex's face, and the only mementoes you'll have of the whole episode will be the columns and your photographs.

Because Kelt and his family were using the private jet, Alex had organised a flight for her on commercial airlines, which had left her exhausted. The noise and heat of a Mediterranean summer in the city beat around her and she was already missing New Zealand, green and crisp and lush.

Doran was home. He came to meet her with a carefully blank face, an expression that turned to alarm and shock when she dropped her luggage and began to weep silently at the sight of him.

'Oh—don't,' he choked and came and took her in his arms, holding her carefully, as if afraid she'd shatter. Awkwardly, he patted her back. 'It's all right, Serina, it's all right. Don't cry—please don't cry. I'm fine, and I'm sorry—I'm sorry I lied to you.'

She gulped back her tears, unable to tell him that they were only partly for him. 'I should hope so,' she said, but her voice wavered. 'I've been sick with worry.'

'I know.' He set her away from him. 'Alex Matthews told me.'

Something in his voice told her that the talk had not been a pleasant one. She remembered Alex's advice— *treat him like an adult.*

'When?'

'He flew into Carathia yesterday, just before I came home.' He pulled a face and said lugubriously, 'We had a long talk, he and I.'

Serina digested this, wondering why Alex hadn't come at least part of the way with her.

No, not *wondering*, she thought bleakly. She knew why. It was his way of showing her that everything was over.

'A long talk?' She tried to conceal her avid interest. 'About what?'

Doran shrugged. 'Oh, everything really. Want something to eat, or coffee?'

'Coffee, thanks. I'm going to have to stay awake until nightfall if I possibly can.'

Chatting of nothing, he made her a drink and, when she'd sat down and picked up her coffee cup, he said, 'It wasn't a pleasant conversation. To put it bluntly, Alex tore strips off me.'

'Did he?' she said neutrally.

He shrugged, looking embarrassed. 'I suppose he had every right to be furious. I hadn't thought of the fallout for Carathia if we actually made it, and Gerd Crysander-Gillan is his cousin.' He frowned. 'Not to mention that his half-sister is Gerd's wife now.'

'I have to admit I didn't think of the possible refugee problem until Alex mentioned it,' Serina said, cautiously feeling her way with Alex's advice very much in mind.

Doran flashed her a relieved look. 'Yes, well, neither had I. And when he told me that the whole scheme had been engineered by the opposition in Montevel—it made me feel *sick*.'

'The opposition in Montevel?' Stunned, Serina stared at him. 'I didn't know there was one.'

'Well, to gain any sort of aid they need an opposition—it's tolerated, but not encouraged.' He leaned forward, face earnest. 'A group of—well, they call themselves freedom fighters and I suppose they are—from the opposition knew they didn't have a chance of gaining power any legitimate way, so some bright spark came up with this idea. They *used* us.'

The coffee bitter in her mouth, she swallowed and said thinly, 'Go on.'

'Apparently, the idea was that we'd stir up a lot of trouble on the border—enough to keep the regime leaders occupied so the freedom fighters could grab power for themselves. They didn't care a bit what happened to us—in fact, Alex didn't say so but, from comments he and Gerd made, I think they were hoping we'd all be killed so they wouldn't have to concern themselves about anybody ever claiming the throne again.' He shrugged. 'I suppose they realised you weren't likely to try, but when I heard that I was very glad you'd stayed in New Zealand.'

Was that why Alex had been so adamant it wasn't safe for her to go back?

'I hope you've realised now that the return of the monarchy in Montevel is not going to happen,' she said, but mildly.

Apparently, she'd struck the right note. Even more seriously, Doran told her, 'Something Alex said made me realise that the people should choose their leaders, not have them imposed on them by—well, by any means. If the Montevellans want a return of the monarchy, then they'll have to get rid of the regime they've got now and ask me if I'll take it on.'

He paused and finished on a wry smile, 'That's if they want me, of course. And I'd want a referendum before I'd accept.'

Thank you, Alex, Serina thought, so grateful she had to put the cup down and take a couple of deep breaths before asking mildly, 'Is there any reason to be concerned about your safety?'

He looked startled. 'Why should there be? We were picked up well before we got anywhere near Montevel, and no one else knows about us.'

'Only those so-called freedom fighters,' she said dryly, 'whose hides might be nailed to the wall if anyone in power in Montevel finds out what they've been up to.'

He gave a short unamused laugh. 'I could almost say it would serve them right. Alex didn't think that would happen. The man they used as our contact—another student at college—has just been told we decided not to go ahead with it.'

'How did he take that?'

He shrugged. 'Oh, called us cowards and so on.'

It was obvious the accusation still stung, but he went on, 'Which was pretty rich, because he stayed safely in Paris while we went off in that yacht. After talking to Gerd and Alex, we all decided we'd been led up the garden path, so we weren't impressed by his ranting. I'm the only one who knows who was actually running the show, and they don't know I know. They'll be certain we can't give them away. As far as anyone is concerned, we've been creating a game.'

Serina said quietly, 'That's a relief. I've been so worried.'

He hesitated, then asked, 'Forgive me for lying to you?'

'Yes.' She looked him straight in the eye. 'Just don't ever do it again.'

'Promise.' He cheered up. 'And, talking about a video game, guess what? One of the big gaming firms wants to have a look at the idea. Alex thinks we should go into discussion with them; he's given us the name of a very good negotiator and says he'll back us!'

Serina swallowed and said brightly, 'That's wonderful.'

He laughed. 'Well, actually, we now have to come up with a proposition,' he said, 'but that's OK. We always viewed it as a game anyway, so it won't take us long to get something together.'

Serina viewed him with wry relief. It was typical of him to put the bad things behind him and move easily onto the next part of his life.

She'd do that too—although, she thought wearily, Alex had been such a magnificent lover she suspected she'd compare any other man with him in the future.

A wave of revulsion at that thought made her get up and start unpacking. It would take her time to get over him.

She could do it.

That night Serina penned what she intended to be a brief thank you letter to Alex. By the time she'd finished it had turned into several paragraphs. She addressed it and sealed it. Tomorrow she'd post it, and that would be an end to everything.

Serina sat down and opened the magazine. Her first column on New Zealand...

How long ago those weeks seemed now. And how foolish she'd been then, how incredibly naïve. A couple of months after she'd got home, she still longed for Alex. She'd somehow assumed she could be like her father, moving from lover to lover without pain.

Instead, she'd been forced to accept that she was her mother all over again—a one-man woman, unable to cut the bonds of her love and move on. She still dreamed of Alex, still opened her email every morning hoping to see something from him, shuffled through the post each day, still devoured the financial pages eagerly, because every so often there was something about him...

Of course he hadn't contacted her. He was a busy

magnate, head of a huge empire, and he probably had another lover now, someone much less inhibited than she was, someone who knew the rules and wouldn't fall in love with him.

She picked up the magazine and flicked through the pages, her brows shooting up when she caught a feature on Rassel, who appeared to have taken his latest inspiration from space travel. If he thought women were going to wear clothes that made them look fat and ungainly, he was sadly wrong...

Pulling a face, she found her page and settled down to check the photographs and read the copy. Halfway through it, she suddenly realised she was staring at the garden at Haruru.

'No,' she breathed, horrified. Perhaps it was an illusion—like her dreams. If she blinked, it might go away.

But it didn't.

She swallowed and read on. 'Oh, God,' she groaned. Alex's name was there.

Wincing, she recalled taking the photograph—the night they'd made love...

She'd emailed the shots to her editor to make sure they'd reproduce well enough for the magazine, stressing they were not to be used.

How had it happened?

Leaping to her feet, she called the editor. Ten minutes of profuse apologies later, she lowered herself into the chair again and looked once more at the photographs.

'All right,' she said aloud. She was tired of longing uselessly, weary of her own futility. This gave her the chance to contact Alex.

She glanced at her watch, did a mental calculation

and relaxed. He'd still be awake—if he was at the homestead.

Cold with apprehension, she dialled the number, only to feel a huge let-down when the housekeeper answered and told her Alex was overseas on a business trip.

'I'm afraid I don't know when he'll be back. Can I get him to ring you when he returns?' she asked politely.

'Thank you,' Serina said, equally politely.

That night she woke in darkness into terror. Hand held over her thudding heart, she couldn't stop shaking. Thick silence enveloped her, pressed down on her chilled skin, froze her.

Slowly, slowly, she turned to face the thing that had hunted her for so long. At first she couldn't see in the darkness around her, but slowly a form coalesced out of it, tall and solid, standing still and watching her.

'Alex,' she breathed in aching supplication.

He said nothing.

She called to him then, frantically trying to break through the cocoon of silence and rejection, and after long moments of silence his lips moved as he said her name.

She heard it in every cell of her body.

He turned away and walked into the darkness. Serina collapsed, sobbing, to her knees, rocking herself back and forward in paroxysms of grief.

Now she understood just what she'd been running from all her life. Herself. The strictures she'd grown up with, the need to be always in control...

Her sexuality.

But, most of all, she'd been fleeing from love.

The shock jolted her fully awake. She was alone in

her own bedroom and she was shivering feverishly, tears burning her eyes.

She should have heeded that dream and avoided love. It hurt so much, so much more than she'd ever imagined it could. At last she understood how her mother had felt with each infidelity, each betrayal of her love for her husband.

Serina pressed her hands to her eyes, wishing she could go back, reclaim her heart, go on with her cool, unemotional life...

And knew she was lying to herself. Whatever the cost, loving Alex was worth it. With him, she'd discovered her own blossoming sexuality, a vividness to life that would fade, but that she'd remember.

She woke the next morning with a headache and during the morning found herself flinching at the noise that poured in from the street. Memories flooded through her of Haruru, fresh and green and fragrant with flower scents, the faint tang of the sea, the clear light...

She felt a longing that was physical, an ache in her heart for the place and the man...

After lunch she'd have a nap, she promised herself as she tidied and cleaned the apartment. Surely that would banish the lingering miasma of the dream.

The doorbell rang. Biting back a sigh, she walked across to the door and opened it.

And there was Alex, tall and dominating and very controlled—except for eyes as cold as a polar winter.

'Oh, dear God,' Serina said, stark fear stopping any logical thought.

'Surely you expected me?' he enquired, all smooth menace. 'Invite me in, Serina.'

She wasn't afraid of him—she was *not*! Stepping

back, she held the door open. And she wasn't ashamed of her apartment, either. It was all she could afford, and she'd made it as pleasant as she could.

He didn't even look around. That lethal gaze was fixed on her, sending a shiver scudding the length of her spine.

'No, I didn't expect you,' she told him, aching with love for him. 'I've only just seen the magazine. I'm sorry. It was a mistake.'

'It certainly was.' He paused, then added softly, 'Your mistake.'

It was then that Serina knew she was never going to stop loving this man. *Never.* She'd go to her grave loving him.

And, judging by the look on his face, that could happen sooner rather than later. In spite of his cold anger, the dull heaviness of the past few months lightened, miraculously lifting her spirits. She had to stop herself from devouring his face with loving eyes.

Instead, she asked spiritedly, 'Have you contacted the editor?'

'Of course. She apologised. For about half an hour in a mixture of French and English.' His tone told her he didn't believe in the sincerity of the apology.

'As I do.' She added, 'Alex, it was my fault for sending those first photographs to her. I have no idea how they got into the magazine—and she doesn't seem to know either—but, believe me, neither of us deliberately organised it.'

'You promised me that they wouldn't be used.' He paused, then added, 'And my name is there too.'

'I know,' she said wretchedly. 'I'm so sorry.'

Eyes narrowed, he said abruptly, 'Have you missed me?'

Serina felt her jaw drop. 'What?' she asked so faintly she could barely hear her own voice.

'You heard,' he said determinedly and came towards her, his face dark and set.

Breath blocked in her throat, eyes widening, she couldn't move. He stopped a few inches away from her and looked down with blazing, steel-sheen eyes. 'Because I've missed you,' he said quietly. 'Every day, every minute, every second—as though an essential part of me has been torn away. Damn it, Serina, I've waited over a year for you—and when at last you came to me, it was—sheer joy. Like nothing I've ever experienced. But then you did this.'

Consumed by incredulous joy alloyed by bewilderment, she fixed on the one thing she could process. 'I did not,' she blazed, careless of the fact that she, who never lost control, had finally and completely lost it. 'I don't lie—and if you can't accept my word on this, then—then—'

She stopped as the import of what he'd actually said sank in. 'What do you mean—you've waited a year for me?'

Savagely, he said, 'Waited for you to see me, of course—not as a substitute for Gerd, not as a temporary lover, but the man who—'

He stopped. Serina froze, unable to speak, unable to even mentally articulate a thought. Her whole future depended on the next few moments, she thought dazedly, yet she couldn't speak.

Roughly, his hands clenched at his sides, he said, 'Well, *say* something.'

'What?' she finally managed to choke out.

He seemed to relax. The frozen fire of his eyes warmed and a set smile tugged at the corners of his mouth. 'You could try saying that you missed me.'

She nodded.

Then he laughed and caught her in his arms and kissed her, and suddenly...it was all right.

No, she thought, every fear and inhibition evaporating as his mouth came down on hers, it wasn't just all right; it was marvellously, wonderfully, exhilaratingly *perfect*.

Opening her mouth to his ravenous demand, she melted into Alex's kiss, so completely happy in that moment that she didn't hear the door open behind them, or see Doran stand there, dumbfounded.

However, through the roaring of her impetuous heart in her ears, she did hear her brother say, 'Ah— OK, I think I'd better go out and come in again.'

Alex broke the kiss and said something she was glad she didn't understand. Above her head, he said curtly, 'You have extremely bad timing, Doran. Get the hell out of here.'

Her brother laughed. 'I think I'd better stay and ask you what your intentions are.'

'Doran!' Serina managed in a horrified croak.

'I'm planning to marry her and make her extremely happy. Any objections?'

'Hell, no,' Doran told him cheerfully. 'Right, I'll leave you to it, then. Serina, I'll be back some time tonight.'

Serina tried to tear herself free from Alex's arms, only to find them tightening around her. She looked up into his face and said in a low, furious voice, 'You'd better ask *me* for an answer, not my brother.'

He looked down at her, his eyes gleaming, and said, 'I know what your answer is going to be. You're going to tell me to go to hell, and then you're going to marry me and have my children and love me for the rest of your life—but not as much as I love you.'

Her anger fled, leaving her shaking with such a wild mixture of emotions she had no idea of what to say or how to feel. Dimly, she heard the door close behind Doran.

She looked up and saw something in Alex's eyes she'd never seen there before—a fierce tenderness. Her heart stopped, then started again jerkily and, to her shock and dismay, she felt hot tears start to her own eyes.

'Don't,' he said in an anguished voice. 'My dearest girl, my darling, don't—please, don't cry.'

But she wept until finally she calmed enough to say, 'Why did you wait so long?'

'At first—' He kissed the top of her head and then her forehead. In a voice roughened by emotion he said, 'I waited for a year after Gerd's coronation because I didn't know how you felt about him. If you'd loved him—or even banked on being his wife—'

'I didn't,' she interrupted swiftly. 'Not either of them—in fact, about a month before Rosie erupted into his life, I told him that, although I liked him enormously, I didn't really feel it was a good idea for us to get too closely linked because it wasn't going anywhere!' She lifted her head and scowled at him. 'You could have asked Gerd.'

He said, 'I did. Gerd wouldn't discuss his relationship

with you but he did say you'd indicated that you weren't interested in him.'

'So why—'

Alex shrugged. 'I wondered if you'd realised he didn't feel for you what he should, and were driven by pride to call it off. So I decided to give you a year.'

Serina made a small sound of exasperation. 'As for *seeing* you—I did that right from the start. Believe me, Gerd wasn't the only one to fall in love at his coronation ball.'

'You could have given me some indication,' he said tersely.

'Would you have believed me?'

Unusually, he hesitated before admitting with a wry smile, 'I suppose I'm not accustomed to people I love staying around for long; my mother died, my father was rarely there, I really didn't get to know Rosie until I grew up. Some time when I was quite young I must have decided that love meant pain. When it hit me I was—afraid…'

Serina hugged him fiercely. 'I know. That's how I felt too—that terror that loving someone meant being hurt by them. But it made no difference—I loved you from the very first.' She stopped, then said starkly, 'I'll love you until I die.'

His arms tightened around her. 'My dearest Serina.' And kissed her—not with the intense passion of a few minutes previously, but with such gentle tenderness that her heart filled with hope.

Against her brow he said, 'I wish I hadn't waited before coming. I think—I suspect it was the fear that your warmth and charm and love would dissipate with distance and time. When I saw that photograph—and my name—I grabbed at anger, because anger is much safer. I didn't want to come to you as a supplicant. But that's what I am.'

'And you came,' she said, shaken to the core.

'I couldn't stay away.' He said it harshly, as though owning to a weakness, and then again, but this time simply, with a kind of awe. 'I feel—stripped,' he said unevenly. 'Filled with such intense happiness because you love me, yet exposed, as though everything I've based my life on until now has been taken from me, and all I have to offer you is myself.' He gave a sudden mirthless laugh. 'And I feel that's not enough.'

'It's everything,' she told him, her voice trembling, unable to smile in spite of the fierce joy that shone through her, washing away the past weeks of pain and grief and longing in a torrent of delight and peace. 'Alex, I love you so much—it's been misery.'

He held her out a little. 'Would you have come to me?'

She said, 'I was going to ring you tonight to apologise for your garden being used in my column.' This time she managed a smile, one that glimmered with mischief and love and such intensity that Alex felt his heart contract. 'I was going to suggest that somehow we should get together to discuss the situation...'

They were married on the beach outside the bach, with only their family and best friends around them. Alex had managed to fend off the insistent clamour of the media, his influence making sure that none of the helicopters in the country were hired to take photographs of the wedding.

As she dressed in the homestead under Rosie's supervision, Serina felt such joy well in her that she had difficulty holding back the tears.

'Hey, that's enough of that—apart from wrecking your eye make-up, it's friends and family who cry at weddings, not the bride,' Rosie told her briskly and hugged her, careful not to disturb her short, exquisite wedding dress and veil.

She stood back and surveyed her with a slight frown. 'You look—radiant,' she said on a sigh. 'And I'm glad you decided to wear your tiara. Little Nora is going to be ecstatic. It was a lovely thought on your part to ask her to be your flower girl.'

'Alex insisted on replacing the stones with real diamonds,' Serina said.

'Of course he did,' Rosie said practically, and beamed at her. 'It's great to see you both so happy. Alex is going to take one look at you and know he's the luckiest man in the world today. Welcome to the family, Serina.'

It was a radiant day too—a soft winter day with a blue, blue sky and the sea hushing quietly a few feet away. Doran, outrageously handsome in his wedding gear, gave Serina away and together she and Alex stood side by side and pledged their troth.

And later, when everyone had gone, they made love in the bach and then lay in each other's arms and talked quietly.

'Why did you want to have the first night of our honeymoon here?' he asked quietly into her hair.

'Because this is where I found you, and myself too.' She sighed and hid a tiny yawn against his bare shoulder. 'I'm going to love spending the rest of our honeymoon in your house in Tahiti, but tonight is perfect...'

She no longer cynically supposed that this transcendent joy would fade after a couple of years; she knew now that other emotions—deeper, stronger, more intense as the years went by—would join it, adding to a happiness that seemed almost too great to bear.

With Alex she was completely safe—as safe as he was with her. Together, she thought dreamily, there was nothing they couldn't face down and win.

Smiling, she whispered his name and slid into sleep, secure in the protection of their love.

Harlequin Presents

Coming Next Month

from **Harlequin Presents®**. Available August 30, 2011

Coming Next Month

from **Harlequin Presents® EXTRA**. Available September 13, 2011

Visit www.HarlequinInsideRomance.com
for more information on upcoming titles!

HPECNM0811

REQUEST YOUR FREE BOOKS!

2 FREE NOVELS PLUS
2 FREE GIFTS!

New York Times *and* USA TODAY *bestselling author*
Maya Banks presents a brand-new miniseries

PREGNANCY & PASSION

When four irresistible tycoons face
the consequences of temptation.

Book 1—ENTICED BY HIS FORGOTTEN LOVER

Available September 2011 from Harlequin® Desire®!

Rafael de Luca had been in bad situations before. A crowded
ballroom could never make him sweat.

These people would never know that he had no memory
of any of them.

He surveyed the party with grim tolerance, searching for
the source of his unease.

At first his gaze flickered past her, but he yanked his attention back to a woman across the room. Her stare bored
holes through him. Unflinching and steady, even when his
eyes locked with hers.

Petite, even in heels, she had a creamy olive complexion.
A wealth of inky-black curls cascaded over her shoulders
and her eyes were equally dark.

She looked at him as if she'd already judged him and
found him lacking. He'd never seen her before in his life.
Or had he?

He cursed the gaping hole in his memory. He'd been
diagnosed with selective amnesia after his accident four
months ago. Which seemed like complete and utter bull.
No one got amnesia except hysterical women in bad soap
operas.

With a smile, he disengaged himself from the group

around him and made his way to the mystery woman.

She wasn't coy. She stared straight at him as he approached, her chin thrust upward in defiance.

"Excuse me, but have we met?" he asked in his smoothest voice.

His gaze moved over the generous swell of her breasts pushed up by the empire waist of her black cocktail dress.

When he glanced back up at her face, he saw fury in her eyes.

"Have we *met?*" Her voice was barely a whisper, but he felt each word like the crack of a whip.

Before he could process her response, she nailed him with a right hook. He stumbled back, holding his nose.

One of his guards stepped between Rafe and the woman, accidentally sending her to one knee. Her hand flew to the folds of her dress.

It was then, as she cupped her belly, that the realization hit him. She was pregnant.

Her eyes flashing, she turned and ran down the marble hallway.

Rafael ran after her. He burst from the hotel lobby, and saw two shoes sparkling in the moonlight, twinkling at him.

He blew out his breath in frustration and then shoved the pair of sparkly, ultrafeminine heels at his head of security.

"Find the woman who wore these shoes."

Will Rafael find his mystery woman?
Find out in Maya Banks's passionate new novel
ENTICED BY HIS FORGOTTEN LOVER
Available September 2011 from Harlequin® Desire®!

HDEXP0911